KINDNESS & HAPPENSTANCE

A SHORT STORY COLLECTION

T J BAINZ

CONTENTS

THE SISTER, SHE APPROACHES

WHEN THE CRYING finally did stop, it was only to be replaced by dampened sobbing.

The breaths inward.

And outward.

In and out. In and out.

The frayed, over-washed, woollen blanket was scratchy against Daniel's bare chest. He had always liked to sleep in only his underwear. But this blanket made it an impossible task. The electrical heater which he'd set up on the floor was blowing too-hot air at his shins, but it seemed an almost *monumental* quest to actually crawl out of bed and amend the situation.

Daniel's tongue, almost operating on an unconscious plane, dawdled over the roof of his mouth. Feeling the stringy, burned skin there. Tasting a little blood. Just like always happened, he had been all too eager for the pizza he had prepared. He had thrust the molten cheese into his mouth a good minute or two early, giving it not a chance to cool.

If Daniel breathed in deeply, he could still *smell* the cheesy topping.

And it sent a quiver down his spine.

Sniff. Sniff. Sniff.

Nose-blow.

Sniff.

Sniff.

Sniff-sniff.

When Daniel had overheard the stories of the breakup of his older sister's marriage, he had gone somewhat against the grain of his established, cold, standoffish personality—the one which he named, in his own mind, 'Public Profile'. He had invited his sister to stay.

He had expected her to refuse.

But she'd said yes.

And once she had said yes, it was really the least that he could do to offer her *his* bedroom.

Another offer she'd accepted.

It *was* Christmas, after all.

That had seen him relegated to the tiny guest room inside of which Daniel kept cardboard box after cardboard box of model aeroplanes.

The room in which he lay now.

The air here smelled strongly of epoxy glue. Across the room, in the silhouette of the darkened room, he could make out his modelling desk. His current model—an Avro Lancaster PA-474, more *colloquially* known as the 'Lancaster Bomber'—sat perched on the desktop. Beneath the switched-off high-wattage lamp. The model was, like the others in the boxes, an old-style type made out of balsa wood.

Year upon year, Daniel had accumulated the aeroplanes. It had moved beyond a hobby, he understood that, and he had no shame in admitting—if only to himself—that it had, well and truly, crossed the threshold to become a full-blown *obsession*.

Ever since Daniel had been born, it seemed, he'd strived for what he had now.

A house to call his own: small but *something*.

A thriving dental practice.

. . . And yet, it was the same old story, that old *cliché* . . . 'something was missing'.

When Daniel set his mind to the matter, he often came upon that old intangible 'company', and what *did* that mean anyway? Since if he was *really* lonely he might get himself a dog, or a cat. And if he could stand having animals in the house, either of those might've been an option.

The truth was, he could hardly stand other *humans* in his house.

So what chance would an animal have?

As Daniel would drive back home, the scent of disinfectant clinging to the suit he wore all day beneath his dentist's apron, he would often lose himself in the dotted white lines which swept beneath his car.

He wondered if it *wasn't* company.

He wondered if it wasn't entirely *something else*.

He wondered if it wasn't just *time*.

Daniel turned over in bed. He faced the wall.

Closed his eyes.

Off, in the further reaches of his house, he heard a double-barrelled *cough-cough*, followed by a long silence. He drifted off to sleep.

Like always, Daniel woke up at half six in the morning without the aid of an alarm clock. His shins felt unbearably sweaty. He sat up in bed—easier said than done since it didn't have a headboard—and gazed down at his body covered with the blanket.

He soon saw the reason for his sweatiness: the heater.

He looked to it there—still *click-clicking* away to itself in a way that he'd long ago grown used to.

He swivelled onto the edge of his mattress, reached over and flipped the switch. It died with a slightly sad, downbeat *whirr* of its fans and Daniel felt the unbearable heat throbbing through his shins come to an end. He breathed in the air—the *morning* air; his favourite kind—and then got himself up and shoved off to the kitchen.

Daniel pulled the curtains open to see that it was still dark outside.

That the trees in his front garden were still ghostly shapes as night retreated.

He could just about make out the amber glow of sunrise on the horizon.

It'd be here soon.

Day would be here soon.

Standing on the cool kitchen tiles in nothing but his boxer shorts, Daniel heard a toilet flush in the distance of his house. He turned around, taken off guard by this sound for a brief second. Then he remembered that his sister had come to stay.

That she'd come to stay for the entirety of Christmas.

But that didn't mean Daniel wouldn't have time to build his aeroplanes.

Between his emergency appointments down at the dental clinic.

Daniel stuck the kettle onto boil, laid a pair of mugs down on the kitchen counter, prepped the cafetiere with a healthy dosage of Colombian coffee then battened down the hatches, taking a seat at the table.

Waiting.

To . . . how did they say? . . . 'pick up the pieces' . . .

His sister Pauline rounded the doorway. She entered the kitchen wearing what, to Daniel's more or less untrained eye, seemed like a fifties-era nightie: a cool, ice-blue with various cuddly cartoon bears all stamped over it. The nightie came just down to her shins.

Pauline had dark circles beneath both eyes. She walked with her shoulders sagging and her bottom lip looked like it'd been chewed almost to death.

When she slumped down into the chair opposite, she let loose an—*obviously*—long-held sigh. She flinched a little as she made herself comfortable, and then dug her arms about her nightie. "Don't you have any cushions?"

"Uh," Daniel said, eyeing the now-boiling kettle, "in the sitting room?"

Daniel was pouring the boiling water into the cafetiere when Pauline returned bearing a pair of cushions of which she laid one on the seat of the chair and the other at the back.

Then—and only then—she took a seat.

She let loose another sigh as Daniel plunged the coffee.

Daniel breathed in deep, not really knowing where to start with all this.

In the end, he decided to play it safe by saying nothing at all.

"Don't you have *anyone?*" Pauline asked.

"Hmm?" Daniel said, tilting his head back towards her, one of his faint, thoroughly professional *dentist* smiles lining his lips.

"I mean," Pauline said, turning in her now-cushioned chair, resting her arm over the back of it, "you don't have a girlfriend"— she paused momentarily—"a *boyfriend* about?"

Daniel felt the colour rise in his cheeks a little. He poured the coffee into the mugs. "No," he said, "I'm afraid not."

"Great," Pauline said, with another sigh, "then I guess it's just going to be a pair of saddos hanging out for the duration of the Festive Period, huh?"

Daniel passed the black coffee over to Pauline.

When she didn't reach to take it from him, he set it down on the table before her.

She sniffed, then reached up and rubbed at her nose with the heel of her hand. "Don't really like coffee," she said.

"Oh?" Daniel said, having just taken his seat, but now hovering a matter of centimetres above it lest he be called into action.

"S'all right, though," she replied, staring down into the steaming blackness, "I'll drink it."

Well, at least she still had her manners.

If breakfast was a train wreck, then the rest of the day was a full-on air disaster.

Daniel had pencilled in a few activities, of which Pauline would've been welcome to join in with. He had thought of driving off to the shops, to go and do the week's supermarket run, but Pauline had shot that one down, saying something along the lines of her and her—*soon-to-be*—ex-husband always ordering the groceries in. She saw no merit in such a wasteful task.

Or a 'hiding to nothing', as she had put it to Daniel.

Driving along in his car, feeling at his most peaceful since his sister had arrived, Daniel considered that—in retrospect—it was nice his sister had stayed home. He, for one, actually quite enjoyed the supermarket-run. There was something oddly *mechanical*, something strangely *unique* in going to a place which never really seemed to change except in the slightest of ways. Perhaps it was how prices would change fractionally, from one week to another, or how the faces of the staff—strangely familiar after his weekly visits—would sort of hang in his mind for literally *seconds* after he'd paid for his shopping.

He'd think about where they might have been born.

And what had brought them here.

And how they had *ended up* working in a supermarket.

But this quiet time was soon at an end when Daniel swooped his car back into the driveway of his house. While he'd been out at the shops, he'd actually felt just a touch guilty in wishing that—*just perhaps*—his sister's mid-range, beige convertible would no longer be in the drive. That he would return to his kitchen, laden down with shopping bags, to discover a handwritten note on the table. Pauline apologising for her abrupt exit, but that she'd had an eleventh-hour reconciliation with her ex, and that she wished Daniel a *Very Merry Christmas* and he wasn't to feel too put out by anything she'd said . . . but, no, she was still there.

As Daniel set about putting the shopping away—the cans into

their cupboards, and the vegetables into their special drawer in the fridge—he couldn't help noticing that, as Pauline sat at the kitchen table, she had a bottle of brandy sitting before her. And he could've *sworn* that said bottle had been unopened when he'd last eyeballed it, in the cupboard.

Now, though, it was easily half-drunk.

Was this how people acted during breakups?

. . . If so, he really hoped that he'd never have a meaningful relationship in his life.

Turning to drink really *was* the pits.

Perhaps the whole scene wouldn't have been so bad if it hadn't been for the time: a few minutes past two in the afternoon. And while Daniel was dressed, as always, in a smart-casual combination of a crisp, white shirt, jeans and well-polished suede shoes; Pauline was still in her nightie. The one she had slept in the night before. The one she had *breakfasted* in that morning.

But Daniel said nothing at all.

He just busied himself with making order of his small nook of the world.

And then, seeing his sister beginning to wobble away on the kitchen chair, he sidled off to the spare room and set to work on the Avro Lancaster PA474.

It was really starting to come together.

As often happened when Daniel sat himself down for some *serious* modelling, he completely lost track of time. Indeed, when he came around to his surroundings—*so to speak*—he noticed how it was, once again, dark out. And how the long winter's night was once more upon the world.

Upon Great Britain, anyway.

He removed his modelling glasses: the ones with small magnifying glasses embedded into the lenses, and laid them down on the desktop, in the way which the manual for caring for the glasses specifically prohibited. He rubbed at his eyeballs, listening to them squeak a little in their sockets, and then he got himself up to his feet, a slight yawn breaking through his lips.

When he looked to his watch, he was surprised to see it had gone seven at night, and he supposed he'd better get himself in order if there was to be any dinner to be had.

At first he couldn't locate his sister.

Pauline was nowhere to be seen.

Not in the sitting room; with the plastic Christmas tree he popped up out of a box every year, and tastefully decorated with white lights. Nor was she in the kitchen, the bottle of brandy now depleted to around a quarter full.

Daniel located the screwcap top for the bottle of brandy, and he did it back up. After he'd replaced the bottle in the cupboard, he set his sights on the rest of the house.

His final search area was his bedroom—the room where Pauline was staying.

He probably wouldn't have bothered to look inside if the door hadn't already been open a crack, but, since it was, he saw no harm in doing so.

There she was—*his sister*—nightie hoiked up to her calves, lying on the screwed-up duvet, lightly snoring away. Her left arm dangled down the side of the bed, and her shoulders rocked up and down with rhythmic breathing. Supposing that—perhaps—he had picked up something of her demeanour from the duration of her stay so far, Daniel allowed himself a slight sigh.

Then he brought the door shut.

Daniel made himself the most delightful of onion-and-cheese quiches for dinner.

And ate it alone.

Not even the End Times would wake Pauline.

Or so it seemed.

That night, Daniel was called out for emergency surgery. As always with these things, his mobile phone awoke him in the early hours with a somewhat smug *buzzing* across his bedside table. When Daniel got up to go make himself a quick cup of instant coffee, he couldn't quite believe his eyes.

What he saw before him.

The kitchen.

His *beautiful* kitchen!

What had once been a well-ordered, sensible space—everything in its right location, labelled, tagged, and obvious as to its place in this small section of the universe—was nothing short of a . . . well . . . a complete *mess.*

There was milk all over the floor.

One gigantic puddle, it seemed, which Daniel sourced as coming from the fridge.

Dribbling down through the slit.

Tin cans, cereal packets, tea bags; all strewn about the floor.

Knowing that time was of the essence, that he needed to deal with this *after* he'd got through with the surgery, he boiled up his coffee, took it with him in the car, and went to work.

Upon returning home, he was surprised to feel a sensation bubbling through his blood. A kind of *shaking.* While he'd been in surgery, the dental nurse—Rebecca—had slipped him several half-asleep, unbelieving sidelong glances. Those glances which silently suggested that he'd been drinking. Because *how else* was Daniel to account for the uncontrollable shaking which took hold of him at least three times during the procedure, and which forced him into pulling back from whatever manoeuvre he'd been planning.

But he *hadn't* been drinking.

And, what was more, he was certain—from the stories he overheard at conferences—that he was one of the few who never *ever* even thought twice about indulging in alcohol while on call, even over the Festive Period. He thought it a touch remarkable, all things considered, that he managed to park his car up in the driveway without any incident. And how he managed to alight, his whole body trembling, without swinging the driver's door into the side of his sister's car. By the time he had crossed the threshold, stood in the front hall, he was ready to run the warpath.

But then he heard the sobbing.

Again.

Faint, and low, and *sad* . . .

In a moment, it disarmed him.

And, after giving himself as cold a shower as he dared on a winter's night such as this, he slipped his aching body in between the spare-room bedsheets and drifted away to sleep.

His mind piecing together imaginary models of aeroplanes.

The next day Daniel got himself up out of bed by about midday.

As if by magic, the kitchen was cleaned up.

That wasn't to say that it was *exactly* as it had been before Pauline had gone on the rampage, but it was certainly *passable*. He could tell Pauline had at least put *some* effort into attempting to piece the place back together so that it *resembled* the order Daniel had forced upon it. And that seemed enough not to rekindle the rage he had felt throbbing through him the night before.

He settled himself down to eat a bowl of cereal, from the packet which had—*clearly*—been uncrumpled from where it had lain on the floor the night before. Although he was sure that he'd got over his mood swing, he couldn't help but find the cereal, those wheaty flakes, devoid of any sort of flavour or sustenance. They might as well have been made from cardboard.

Even the aroma of his long-awaited coffee had no effect on him.

It neither perked him up or satisfied his craving for its dry taste.

What was more, even though Daniel had set the thermostat to a steady twenty degrees, he felt as if there was a draught blowing about the house. And though Daniel didn't shudder from the cold, he certainly *felt* cold inside.

Empty.

Was this what people talked about when they said things like, 'cold, hard decision-making', or 'giving it the thousand-foot view'?

Had he made up his mind.

Was that why he was so diffused.

So *unangry*?

Because there was only one thing for it now, and Daniel knew it for himself too.

His sister had to leave.

But as Daniel waited patiently at the kitchen table, tapping through the front pages of the media outlets on his tablet—and feeling none of the words actually managing to bite his mind— Pauline didn't deign to show herself. He thought, several times, about awakening her.

That might be the best approach.

. . . But, and this was the strange thing, given the decision he had apparently come to, he thought that it might be *encroaching* on her personal space to go knock on her bedroom door.

So he continued to sit.

Waiting . . . *forever waiting* . . . like some sort of faithful dog.

When Pauline finally *did* show herself, it had gone—by Daniel's wristwatch—quarter past three in the afternoon. And she hadn't had an emergency surgery to deal with in the middle of the night.

She slipped Daniel a slight smile, and he read those unfocussed eyes of hers. Seeing it almost every day in one of his morning patients, before they opened their mouths and confirmed it with their rancid breath—thank *God* for his facemask—he knew that it indicated a 'hangover'.

An *overindulgence.*

And Pauline had *certainly* overindulged the night before.

As Pauline stood with her back to Daniel, turning on the kettle to make herself some tea—*without* asking Daniel if he'd like a cup —he decided that the time was right . . . that he needed to strike the blow quickly and without mercy.

"Um, Paulie?" Daniel said, already feeling the muscles in his throat constrict and his voice wavering all over the shop.

No response.

"It's about last night—about the kitchen."

Again, nothing.

"The thing is, when I invited you here, asked if you'd like to stay, I thought that you would, well"—Daniel searched for *some* expression that might not make him sound like either of his, deceased, parents—"play by the rules," he finally got out, already feeling himself wince internally.

Pauline kept her back to Daniel.

The kettle was boiling now.

Steam pouring from the plastic spout.

Something about the scene was intimidating.

But Daniel tried—*hard*—not to let it bother him.

"And I know that you did a good job in cleaning up the place—I mean to say, if I hadn't seen the state of the kitchen last night, then I never would've guessed how . . . how it had looked . . ."

That last part was a lie, seeing as Daniel would've noticed so much as a fork out of place in his kitchen. Although his memory wasn't as good as it had been back when he'd been a young buck, his extraordinary—and, some might say, totally superfluous—talent for recalling the exact state and order of his kitchen was very much intact.

"Look," Daniel said, deciding that he needed to cut to the quick of this so that he wouldn't end up sounding like a total waffler, "what I want to ask is: isn't there anybody else that you might feel more, uh, *comfortable* staying with over Christmas?" Still seeing that Pauline had her back to him, he cleared his throat and mumbled out a, "Hmm?"

Pauline remained still for a long time.

Many millions of possible scenarios passed through Daniel's mind. He wondered if Pauline might seize hold of the kettle handle, popping the plastic lid as she went, toss boiling water over him.

But she didn't.

She just stayed still another few seconds and then—calmly, *quietly*—poured herself out the cup of tea. She left the teabag to brew for about a minute before retrieving it with a spoon and depositing it—without allowing so much as a drop of tea to strike the kitchen floor—in the sink.

She added a splash of milk to her tea then sat down at the table.

Opposite him.

For a long time, she just stared into the mulchy, brown contents of her mug, and it might've been any number of things bobbing about on her mind.

Things that Daniel—*really*—had little-to-no comprehension of either the beginning or ending of.

Finally, she glanced up.

She wasn't crying—there were no *tears* sparkling in her eyes.

In fact, for the first time since she'd been here, in Daniel's home, she looked like she might have sort of pulled herself together. "I'll pack my things," she said.

Her words hung in the air, mingled with the steam from the kettle, the slightly sour odour of milk.

And it was then that Daniel *himself* felt like he might burst into tears.

Daniel let Pauline out at the train station, suitcase in hand, after she had assured him that she had someplace to go—a loose mention about a 'friend' on the other side of the country.

She had claimed that she was in no fit state to drive.

He listened to the car engine idle.

Felt the warm air puffing through the vents.

The slightly *dusty* smell of the car.

And that taste of his cereal, those little bits still stuck between his teeth.

As Daniel watched Pauline disappear inside the station building, he found himself thinking about their childhood together. How had it ended up like this?

With *her* depending on *him*?

He could still recall, all those days, coming home from school only to find his sister sitting about with her friends, in the garden, puffing away at cigarettes while their mother and father were on their way home from work. How many times had he attempted to silently slip in through the front door, set foot on the staircase and haul himself up to his bedroom, where he could be *alone* with his aeroplane models, only to hear their group *cackle*—some utterance about him—and have it follow him into his solitude. In retrospect, he supposed that it was his sister's treatment of him which had led to his ferocity for study. He had no trouble at all sitting in a room alone—for several hours at a time—and 'hitting the books' till he couldn't even remember the outside world any longer.

It had been something of a vicious cycle.

He would arrive home.

Find his sister and her *friends* there—where were those 'friends' now?—and he'd jog his way up to his bedroom, where he could be alone: *protected*.

Where had his sister been when he'd struggled at school?

When he'd been shoved to the ground those countless times?

She had never stuck up for him . . . and yet she had run in all those groups, been *involved* with all those *bullies* scattered throughout the school.

She could have done something.

Just as *he* could do something for *her* now . . . or not.

Daniel placed his hands on the steering wheel, ready to pull out of the Stopping Zone, to drive away from the train station, back home to his model aeroplanes, to his *wondrous* solitude. Back to the Good Life. However, when he curled his fingers about the hand-brake, it felt like he might be trying to push against a concrete block.

A car horn blared behind him.

Daniel glanced back over his shoulder.

Looking—he was *certain*—like a startled rabbit.

What was he doing?

What *was* he doing?

The engine still purring along, Daniel undid his seatbelt. He opened the car door with a vicious *snap*. As he trotted away from his car, he heard somebody yelling obscenities directed at him. But he ignored them. He knew that they couldn't understand.

Because, if he didn't understand himself, then what chance did *they* have?

The train station was packed.

People with suitcases on wheels.

All bundled up in winter coats.

Newspaper stands—was that what they were still called?—and an intangible sense of *urgency* clinging to the entire scene.

Through the crowd, Daniel spotted Pauline's distinctive red cape. He watched her meander through the people. He recalled how—when she'd first pulled up outside his house—she'd put him in mind of Red Riding Hood. Perhaps like one of those *realistic* fantasy tales, with the girl all grown up, and crushed by the problems of day-to-day life.

But Daniel was determined, now, that this wouldn't be one of those.

Determined.

He caught a fair few barrages of abuse from the travellers he bustled through, but nobody tried to stop him. Not even the ticket inspectors on the barrier. He supposed that they were used to seeing desperate people—people who simply *had* to get in touch with the nearly departed . . .

He reached her just as she was about to step onto the train.

When he grasped hold of her shoulder, she spun around, her hand ready to deliver a slap to his cheek. Maybe she'd have had the strength to break his jaw. But, when she saw who it was, her expression melted away. She withered a touch. Her lips traced words.

They just never made it into sound.

Before Daniel knew quite what he was doing, he wrapped his arms about her, clutched her to his chest. And he could feel the convulsion of her sobs.

As he propped his arm about her shoulders, dragging her luggage with his other hand, he couldn't help himself from whispering in her ear, "We'll have a Merry Christmas together—I'm sure of it."

HEAVY HANGS THE HAMMER

1

THERE ARE FEW THINGS worse than a leisurely Sunday morning lie-in being ruined by senseless hammering.

At least Terri thought as much as she lay on her stodgy mattress with a long-wilted pillow clutched over her ears. It was her neighbour—Paul, was it?—again at his DIY far too early for any *healthy* living person to tolerate.

With a droopy eye, Terri glanced to the neon-lit alarm clock on her bedside table. She saw that it had just gone six thirty in the morning. She drew in a deep breath, one of those ones which threatens to explode at any second, and she tossed off her duvet, left it in a crumpled-up heap on the floor.

As she threw her over-washed dressing gown over her bare shoulders—she wore a strappy nightdress to bed—she felt the coarse material rub up against her skin, and it made her shiver just a little.

There were few things she enjoyed less than having to give the neighbour a bollocking on a weekend.

She slipped out through the side door of her house.

The wooden-slatted garden fence was one of those which she'd often thought was far too small to be of any use. It was one of those which came up only to knee-height, and so only offered a sort of notional boundary between the two properties rather than any sort of *tangible* privacy.

If only she could move someplace else.

If only she could get herself shot of these neighbours.

But, she supposed, on days like these, the knee-high fence came in handy. Because, with only a neat step over it—no doubt those hundred squats she did every weekday morning paying off—she was on the neighbours' property and staring right into the garage

—its door open, of course—and looking right down the crack of Paul's(?) particular brand of builder's bum.

She cleared her throat in between his percussive hammering.

He froze for a moment, as if she had scared the wits out of him, and then he gazed back over his shoulder at her. When he did look at her, he was grinning—that smile full of abscessed teeth and, no doubt if she dared take a couple of steps closer, replete with halitosis.

Terri instructed herself to be calm. She wasn't going to lose her rag with him. That was the very worst thing that could go on with a neighbour. After all, she had to see him pretty much every day . . . they *always* seemed to run into one another.

"Do you know what time it is?" Terri said.

Paul(?) cocked his head to one side, then he scratched away at his bald scalp.

Terri watched a few flakes of dandruff float down as serenely as a scattering of leaves falling from the branch of an oak tree in autumn. She watched said flakes land on the shoulder of his sun-faded, red polo shirt and, for a couple of moments, she was almost hypnotised by them.

" 'Time' ?" he said, as if they were having an impromptu discussion on its abstract definition.

Terri supposed she should help him out. "Six thirty. Saturday *morning*," she said, taking particular care to stress the 'morning' part.

Paul(?) pouted at her. His hammer, which had a fluorescent orange rubber grip, hung down at his thigh. He blinked once. Twice. And then, taking Terri completely off guard, tears sprang from the corners of his eyes and rolled down his cheeks. He bowed his head, averting her gaze and sobbed away into his chest.

Terri felt her chest tighten. A chill run through her blood. What was it about her and criers? It didn't matter where she saw them: random people on the street, somebody at the office bawling their eyes out—normally their secretary, Rachel—even when she was watching a film, she always had exactly the same reaction.

She wanted to help them.

Wanted to be *close* to them.

It was something which she couldn't control at all.

She felt herself quivering inside, and she took a couple of steps towards Paul(?).

As she got closer to him, he gave a couple of long—*hard*—snorts and glanced up at her briefly. She saw how his tears made his eyeballs glisten. And seemed to bring out the grey tones of his irises. Just like any self-respecting crier assistant, Terri had a whole bundle of tissues in the pocket of her dressing gown. What she had been thinking when she'd stuffed them in there, what sort of situation she'd imagined herself coming up against and arriving in some encounter with a crier, she really had no clue.

But the fact remained.

The tissues *were* there.

She brought out a couple of them, flattened out the creases that she'd pressed into them while they'd been in her pocket, and she handed them over to Paul.

Paul took them with a slight smile, blew his nose hard—twice—and then swallowed. As he held the tissues in his fist, Terri caught the impression—just for a single second—that he might be considering handing the tissues right back to her.

But he, apparently, thought better of it.

As Paul got himself together, Terri risked a look over his shoulder, looked into the garage, to see what exactly it was that he was working on.

From out of the slight shade that lay over the interior of the garage, she could make out what looked like a door, lying down over one of those pop-up bench thingies: the ones that were generally used, in her own limited knowledge of DIY, for sawing.

She could see that there was a whole series of jagged nails

sticking out from the door in, what seemed to her, like a fairly *dangerous* way.

For a couple of seconds she caught a strange whiff of the fresh —*too early*—morning air, mixed in with the smell of the garage: the cool scent of paint, that soil-like odour of concrete.

When she brought her focus back onto Paul, she could hear the birds striking up around them, rattling out their chirruping little songs. She felt a slight lurch at the base of her gut. That reaction which she knew was suggesting to her, in no uncertain terms, that she should be cooking herself up a black—*very black*—coffee. Already she could taste its bitterness, or maybe she could smell it somehow, from somewhere, some other nutcase neighbour on her street who took some sort of masochistic pleasure from waking up before seven in the morning on a Saturday.

Paul was blabbing something to her, something between a whisper and a grunt. His eyes didn't seem to meet hers for a single second. "Last night," he said. "She took the dog."

" 'The dog' ?" Terri said, it apparently being her turn to echo his words.

He nodded, then swallowed again. He bunched his fist even tighter about the used tissues.

Terri thought hard, could just about remember that she would occasionally hear the *scuttle* of claws on the wooden decking out the back of her neighbours' house . . . out the back of *Paul's* house. It had been a well-behaved dog, though, since she could never recall, not even once, hearing an actual bark.

Then she snapped her mind back to just what this might mean.

Just *why* the neighbour was in tears.

Why the neighbour's wife had taken the dog.

Though she spent most of her days, as a letting agent, reading people, and their problems—said and unsaid—she found that on weekends she had a habit of turning off even the most basic of her reading ability.

Quite simply put, on a Saturday, or a Sunday, for that matter, she was just perhaps a notch above a lobotomised ape in terms of her ability at reading people.

She looked Paul over another time, and, without him having to say anything more, she deduced the issue here. And, never having been one for tact, she spat it right out.

"Your wife's left you?" she said.

Paul gave her a solemn nod.

Terri tried to work out what she was going to do next. Then decided that this was something that was, most likely, best left alone. If it did happen that Paul and his wife were having marital 'issues' then she probably wouldn't be helping out much in her role as the eligible—*very eligible*—spinster next-door.

Before she could excuse herself, though, Paul spoke.

"You, uh," he began, the hammer still hanging down at his side, and scratching the back of his neck with the hand in which he held the tissues, "wouldn't like to come over a bit later for a cup of tea, would you?"

Terri assessed the offer. It seemed good-natured enough. And, under normal circumstances—under *weekday* circumstances—she really wouldn't have had any trouble at all simply rejecting him out of hand. But these weren't normal circumstances. She'd got that whole dizzy weekend feeling about her.

And so, almost unconsciously, she found herself saying, "Okay, Paul, that sounds nice."

Just for a fraction of a second Paul furrowed his brow, pursed his lips. "My name's Peter," he said. "*Pete* if you like."

Though at work Terri prided herself for her ability to recall names at an almost autistic level, she couldn't say the same for what, for want of a better term, might've been described as her 'social life'.

She felt herself reddening just a little in her cheeks. And then she pinned on a smile and tried out his name, "Okay, Pete," she said, "I'll see you a little later."

And, just like that, Terri skittered back indoors.

2

I T WAS AROUND Terri's third coffee—and about eleven thirty in the morning—when she realised what a great mistake she was making.

And how she was breaking one of *many* cardinal rules she kept for herself.

Even out there, in the driveway, she'd explained to herself how she *certainly wouldn't*—*not under any circumstances*—get herself involved in whatever marital knot had worked its way in between Paul . . . *Pete* . . . and his wife.

But, then again, she had accepted now.

If she backed out of it she'd have to come up with a reason.

That'd be for the best, though.

Better for her to stay out of this whole thing altogether.

She downed the dregs of the coffee, placed the stained white cup in her porcelain sink, and then she strutted on over to the hook where her cordless phone hung off. Up there, on the wall, on a good thirty—or, goodness, were there as many as forty?—scraps of paper, corners all peeled back, and yellowed from their exposure to the sun, she scanned for the name of their neighbours, and the phone number beneath.

She found it after a brief search—the Brookys, apparently—and she read off the number she'd scrawled there in her flowery handwriting . . . in blue ink, for what it was worth.

The phone chirped in her ear several times and then she heard a dampened—almost *throttled-sounding*—voice on the line.

"Hello?"

"Pete?" she said, gazing out the window to her flowering garden—the garden which her gardener, who she never saw since he came while she was at work, and who she had termed 'The Yeti', mainly to herself, had kept in pristine condition. "It's Terri here," she said. "From next door."

"Hmm?" he said, and though she wasn't totally one-hundred-per-cent sure whether or not it was a question, she decided that it was best for her to crack on.

"About the tea today," she said.

" 'The tea' ?" he replied.

"Yes, you see, the issue I've been having . . . well, you see, I was just looking over my calendar, right now, actually, and I found that I'm meant to be meeting a friend."

She screwed up her eyes at that, thinking to herself that, really, she should've been a little more creative . . . but there wasn't much she could do about it now, not now that she'd gone and *said* it.

"Oh?" he said, apparently still not quite catching the significance of this development.

"So," she said, "I'm not going to be able to come round for tea— I mean, I'd already told my friend that I would be meeting her, and, well, between you and me"—she thought for a second about whether or not she should go on, but decided it was for the best —"she's having some real *issues* at the moment, needs a shoulder to cry on, that sort of thing."

She winced, thinking about how she'd put her foot in it.

If Pete decided to start crying over the phone then she'd have a desperately hard time convincing her conscience to simply allow her earthly body to stay put and *not* go on over and see what it was that she could do.

But, it appeared, Pete was finally catching her drift.

"Okay," he said, with that same dampened tone of voice, and then he hung up.

Caught in something approaching shock, Terri held the phone to her neck for a couple of moments. That had been easy. He'd made it so easy for her. She had expected a whole mess of consequences. Had expected him to push her to name an alternative date, no doubt for tomorrow—for Sunday.

But in the end he'd simply hung up on her.

It took a couple of moments for this realisation to leak through her before she allowed herself to smile—long and hard. When she replaced the phone in its cradle, she did so with great vigour, and then she hopped on upstairs to run herself a very long—and very bubbly—bath.

3

O N MONDAY MORNING, after doing her hundred squats, and getting through her shower—along with the other womanly necessities—Terri headed on out through her front door wearing her smart, charcoal-coloured trouser suit, her smooth, leather workbag hanging down limply from her fingertips. She held her flask of coffee tight in her hand as she clacked her way, in her high heels, over the concrete slabs of her garden path and to her waiting hatchback car. She'd just about got to laying her flask of coffee, as she always did, on the roof of the car, shunting her keys into the driver's door, when something caught the corner of her eye. She looked over and squinted, not quite able to believe what she was seeing.

There, lying on his back in his drive, in front of the garage, and still wearing that sun-faded, red polo shirt, and apparently all the rest of his clothes from Saturday, was Pete.

He was staring upwards, up into the overcast, Monday morning sky.

As if Terri was expecting to see a flying saucer bearing down on him, she met his gaze and followed it. But there was nothing out of the ordinary that he was looking at.

At least to her mind, he was staring into mid-air.

She felt her shoulders draw tense. She slipped her mobile out of her bag and checked the time. She was about five minutes ahead of schedule, like always, as she always *designed* it so that if she was to run into any trouble—any trouble at all—she wouldn't find herself in that nightmarish scenario of *arriving late*.

Yes, she had time.

And so, after stuffing her workbag and flask of coffee into her car, leaving them on the passenger seat, she looked over at Pete and said, "Uh, are you all right there?"

Pete remained in his same position and, for a heart-stopping moment, Terri considered the possibility that he might be dead. That, perhaps, he'd gone and had a heart attack and collapsed there in his drive. Maybe she should run inside, go call an ambulance, and she might well have done if she hadn't noted how his chest was rising up against his shirt.

She glanced around herself, as if there might be somebody lurking nearby to take this problem off her hands . . . there wasn't . . . so she approached him.

"Uh, Pete?" she said, her voice sounding much more scared, more *frail* than she had intended it to.

He continued to breathe, but his eyes remained locked on the air directly in front of his nose.

"Would you like some help?" she said.

Still Pete maintained his position, totally unmoved by her words.

She glanced around another time, and found that her only company right at that moment was a tortoiseshell cat crouching—primed—on the edge of one of Pete's flowerbeds.

She turned her attention back to Pete, and then thought to crouch down. "Pete?" she said. "Can you hear me? If you don't speak to me, tell me you're okay, then I'm going to have to call an ambulance."

She thought about this, about how she could quite easily call to work, tell them that she was having an 'issue' with her neighbour. Though she had a client coming in at nine o'clock on the dot, she knew that another of the letting agents would quite happily cover for her. She had covered for them countless times before, after all, and this would be the first time that she had been found wanting in terms of her scheduling . . . she supposed that was what she got for not having a husband, a family, kids . . .

Pete's lips moved, almost imperceptibly, and he murmured

something—something which Terri really had no hope whatsoever of understanding.

"Sorry?" Terri said. "I didn't hear."

He swallowed hard, Terri watched his Adam's apple bob against his throat, and then he tried again, ". . . She took the dog," he said.

Terri looked about them, trying to see if anything—*anybody*—beside the cat might be on the scene to shine some light on this situation.

No luck.

Terri looked back to the garage door, and then said, hoping to take Pete's mind off whatever this crisis was, "What were you hammering on—in there?"

Pete held still for a long while, kept on staring upwards, into mid-air. "A trap."

" 'A trap' ?"

"Hmm," he said.

"A trap for what?"

"For the dog."

Terri felt her heart beat a little faster. She couldn't quite get her head around just what he was talking about. What did he mean that he wanted to make a trap . . . and for his dog? One thing was for certain—though she supposed the penny should really have dropped a couple of minutes earlier—this man, *Pete*, was obviously in need of some psychiatric help.

What else did she think seeing as he'd seemed to have been lying here for a couple of nights and a day?

But, at the same time, she was a little afraid of leaving him here, where he'd—surely—continue to lie in his concrete driveway.

Pete spoke again, and it cut off Terri's train of thought.

"If it comes back," he said.

"What?" Terri said.

"The trap," he said, "it's for if the dog comes back."

"Oh," Terri said, feeling the wrinkles form in her forehead, and at the same time wondering how she might be able to get away from him and to a phone as quickly as she could.

There really wasn't any other option.

She just needed to make a clean break.

Needed to shift herself away from him.

Go and get the phone.

Easy.

Just a matter of getting up . . .

"Terri?" Pete said.

Terri tilted her head down to him. At first she couldn't recall having given him her name, and then she recalled that she *had* . . . that she'd told him her name, at least, over the phone, if he hadn't already known it.

"Yes?" she said. "What can I do?"

"Why didn't you come over for tea, Terri?"

Terri blinked a few times, the overcast day getting suddenly bright. She held her hand up to shield her eyes. "Like I told you, I had a friend to go and meet."

Pete didn't reply.

"Look," Terri said, catching a glance of her phone, and the time, "I've got to go inside for a second, okay? I'll be back in a moment, is that all right?"

No reply.

Terri tested out her resolve. She raised herself back up to a straight-backed position, and then she took a step away from her prostrate neighbour. She shifted towards the side door, the door of her house which led to the kitchen.

"Terri?" Pete said.

"Yes?"

"I know that you lied to me," he said. "I know that you didn't have anybody to meet, you have *nobody* to meet. You live all alone." He paused for what must've been just a moment, but it seemed to stretch out into almost an eternity. "I thought you could do with the company."

Terri felt her throat tightening. Her hands trembled just a little. But she held still. Forced herself not to react at all. Just as she acted every day of her life. She told herself that emotions were for the 'little' people. They were for the people who couldn't keep that *animal* instinct held tightly within themselves from bursting right out.

And she was better than those little people.

Wasn't she?

"I'll be right back," she said, and then stepped over the threshold, and into the kitchen, to the waiting phone.

4

FIFTEEN MINUTES LATER, Terri stood on her front doorstep as she watched the two men wearing white coats lead Pete along with them to their clean white van with the tinted windows. She noticed how one of the men clutched a syringe in his hand which he held down at his side, apparently so that Pete wouldn't notice it there.

But it was clear, at least to Terri, that Pete wasn't in any sort of shape to notice anything so subtle as a syringe.

Or a giant, inflatable fairground mallet, for that matter.

He was a shell of a man.

As she listened to the gentle *rumble* of the ambulance as it pulled away, she waved to the man in the white coat who sat in the front, with the window wound down. Once they'd slipped away from view, Terri stood still there for several moments. She knew that she should be getting to work, that she *needed* to be getting to work. She'd told her boss that she wouldn't be much longer than about an hour late . . . she had another client, after all.

But there was just one thing.

One thing that she needed to check on.

And so she shut the front door behind her and rounded her house, stepping along the wooden fence which divided her property from her neighbour Pete's.

She found herself standing there, before his garage, still shut, as it had been, to her knowledge, since that fateful, early Saturday morning.

As she swept her gaze downwards, along the retractable door, down to the concrete, she saw it. The hammer. Lying there. Its rubber, bright-orange grip. It lay there on the ground, apparently discarded without any further thought required.

Had Pete tossed it there the minute that Terri had cancelled tea? Had he simply given up on his hammering and, in some sort of an impotent rage, allowed the hammer to drop at his feet? And then simply fallen to the ground himself?

She stared a long time at the hammer, fixated on it, trying to scope out any sort of meaning that might have been left attached to it.

But she found nothing.

Only an object.

Just another *thing*.

As Terri was on the brink of turning around, heading off to her car, and to work, she found herself approaching the hammer, heading for it. And, before she knew it, she was stooping down, reaching out for it with her carefully manicured fingernails.

She held it tight in her hand.

She turned it over.

Felt its steady weight.

Gave it a little, playful swing.

And, before she knew it, she was crying—crying *hard*—and it seemed that there was nothing at all in this world that could stop her.

RETURN UNOPENED

D EAR CLARA,

Since you don't return my calls or emails, I thought the only way to explain was in a letter.

It's a bit harder to rip up a letter than to ignore a call or delete an email, isn't it?

One-way conversations are how I've earned my keep all these years, so I should be up to task—if you're willing to give me a fair hearing, of course.

If you were to ask me how it all started, I'd have to begin that wet and dark August afternoon, two years ago.

We pulled into the station and stepped onto the platform. Rain lashed down, soaking my suede coat. When I checked the clock, I realised we had only ten minutes before our connecting train and we hadn't bought a birthday present for Angela, who was meeting us at the other end. Since we just needed *something* I volunteered to dip into the station building and peruse the shops.

There wasn't much choice inside: a café, a post office and a sex shop.

At that time Angela was feeling down, living with us. I just wanted something to make her chuckle. Nothing says: 'I don't care' better than a generic card with some message about being special, and that was why I went into the sex shop and purchased a vibrator. A small, black one on a keychain.

We reunited outside, a hot coffee each, then hurried to catch our train home.

Angela met us at the station. I must admit it was the first time I thought we might work.

That must be difficult for you to hear, but I want to be honest.

On the ride home I thought about throwing the vibrator away, winding down the window and just letting it drop on the road. But I held onto it, keeping it snug in the inside pocket of my jacket.

After dinner, and several glasses of wine, we sat in the sitting room, the TV burbling about in the background. As a family we never made a big deal of birthdays: no cake, perhaps a present or two at a low key moment of the day, even so, when I presented her the gift, I recall my heart drumming, sweat dampening my neck.

Angela squinted at the bag then cocked her head to one side. I thought the entire joke would be lost. But when she unwrapped the vibrator, the corners of her mouth tugged back in a grin—the first in a long time.

Then we all laughed.

Out of relief, more than anything, I clapped my hands and bellowed. No one ever laughed in our house.

That night I fell asleep with a smile on my face.

The weeks passed without further mention of the gift, but I often wondered about it—about what Angela got up to alone. At work I was in pieces, zoning out to a land of daydreams. She consumed me. Then, one day, amongst the rubble of another rehearsal, she visited me at the theatre.

You know my policy on family in the workplace. I remembered all the times you asked for a part in a play: a peasant girl or an anonymous courtesan.

I always fobbed you off, telling you it wouldn't work, that the other actors would get jealous. This was different, though, because no one knew about Angela or that she had any relationship to me. Having her so close, and away from the house, sent a thrill through my veins.

A blood buzz!

I gave her a small part.

Nothing happened between us during the production and once

it finished that was that. We returned to our old context, back to the house. She never asked for another part and I never offered her one. But the seeds were sown. Needless to say, tensions frayed at home—always tricky with more than one women under the same roof!—and Angela left.

And that seemed to be the end of that.

Months flew by and my birthday arrived. The doorbell shook me awake that morning. Once I had fumbled my glasses onto my nose, I ventured downstairs where a package was waiting.

A large one.

No return address, but I recognised Angela's handwriting.

I shuddered with excitement as I lugged it into the laundry room.

Inside the box, nestled in packing foam, was a leather suit and chain. A chill ran through my whole body and it felt like a thousand pairs of eyes were watching me.

Upstairs something stirred.

I shoved the box underneath a cabinet and returned to the kitchen.

You stepped in yawning, still in your dressing gown. You noticed my flushed face, I'm certain. Perhaps now you can add a little meaning to that manic episode. I waited until you had gone out shopping then relocated the present to the garage.

But it remained on the edge of my mind always.

From then on I knew the truth.

I loved Angela.

Those days were the hardest. I just existed, living two lives. If I had been a real man, I would've plucked up the courage, made my decision and left. But I lingered. I conjured half-baked excuses: late rehearsals, early meetings. It was a farce for a year or more.

Then it all came tumbling down.

I was planning to meet Angela that morning, rushing down a bowl of cereal. When you entered with a basket of clean laundry, I noticed one of Angela's thongs on top. I have no idea how it got there, perhaps it fell from one of my trouser pockets.

Fate conspired against us.

Without thinking, I snatched it up.

When you looked me up and down, I swear your eyes scorched my soul. Everything unravelled. You dropped the basket and ran upstairs before I had a chance to explain.

When I returned home from work that night, all my things were in cardboard boxes on the doorstep. I just picked them up and dropped them in my car boot without another glance at the house or a word of goodbye.

Well, that's about the measure of it, I don't want to outstay my welcome. All I wanted to say was that your aunt and I are happy and well.

Please send our apologies to your mother.

To lose a husband and sister in one fell swoop cannot be easy.

Perhaps one day I shall write a play and dedicate it to her, some miserable compensation.

I hope she can find someone to love her.

As ever, your loving father.

Please forgive me.

LAST GIANT

1

IT WAS NIL-NIL in the Cup Final and Peter Jones stood jostling his man, Eric Frankston, in the penalty box. Sweat poured over his cheeks and down the neck of his shirt. He didn't dare to tear his eyes from the ball, in the corner, placed on the cone-shaped white line.

The corner taker smashed the ball in. All around Peter opposition players fought with those on his side. The ball fizzed through the air toward him, coming toward his head. He had it. No way he'd let Frankston get to it. Closer and closer. His heart beat in anticipation.

The ball got about half a metre from his nose. Frankston reached around him and, with his fist at Peter's chest, punched it. The ball curved past Peter and into the corner of the net. Screams and clapping thundered about the stadium.

The referee blew twice on his whistle, a sharp pair of notes in the early evening air, to signal the end of the match. Instantly Peter's teammates crowded the referee, their arms flapping and mouths blabbering out insults. The referee kept his whistle in his mouth and waved them away, shaking his head all the time.

A numbness gripped Peter's chest. Pins and needles jabbed his bones.

How had the referee not seen it? Surely it had been clear to anyone watching that Frankston had used his hand to put the ball into the goal.

Cheated.

But Peter had no energy to complain. It had been a long season and Peter had had an inkling that it might well end like this. Although he hated to admit it, his passion for the game had died. He dropped to his knees, allowing his head to fall into the damp, mud-flecked turf, not caring any more.

For several minutes, he just lay there, face-down, no longer wanting to look at the world.

Someone tapped him on the shoulder.

A group of voices wafted about his brain. He twisted his neck and glanced up.

A journalist loomed over him. He wore a wide smile and held a microphone with a fluffy windshield. "Got some time for an interview, Pete?"

A coldness draped over his whole body. He usually despised interviews, journalists buzzing about him like flies asking endless inane questions, but what difference did it make?

This was it for him.

No longer would he live in a world of cheats and charlatans.

Sometimes he worried about how he would look for the camera, whether he was wearing everything that he'd signed up for in his endorsement contracts.

Once he had forgotten to wear a silver necklace at a press conference. That had cost his agency a hefty breach-of-contract fine. And although no one had got angry with him he could see—behind those plastic smiles—that they were secretly cursing him, thinking he was stupid. When the real truth was that he really didn't care. He wanted to play football.

That was his life.

He got to his feet and brushed a few specks of mud from his white shorts. The journalist jabbed his microphone in his face, cocked his head and looked him in the eye. "Well, quite a bit of late drama there, with the sending off and then the contentious decision to award the corner, followed by your own goal. What was your opinion on the late goal?"

Peter couldn't even be bothered to fight this battle. Despondency just filled his entire being. He shrugged. "Didn't see it."

The journalist chuckled. "You can't be serious. You must have a view on it, since you were marking Frankston. Did you see him handle the ball?"

"It all happened so fast. Sometimes it's difficult to see."

"Still, there are those that think such instances should be taken care of after the game. Do you think the referee will regret the decision to award the goal?"

Peter's gaze drifted beyond the journalist to the players' tunnel, where a series of jostlings had broken out among his and the opposing team.

Handbags.

Toys getting thrown out of the pram.

He was surprised that, after all this time, his team mates really cared.

Why not just throw in the towel?

"Peter?" the journalist said, then, still smiling, "We don't have much time. They're going to be wanting to get on with the ceremony before too long. We'll have to clear off the pitch. Do you have any comments on the officials' performance during the match?"

"No."

The journalist bobbed his head then looked back at his producer. When he turned to Peter once more, the corners of his mouth seemed to strain to support his smile. "All right, I understand that it's an emotional time at the end of the match, we'll just give you a few moments peace before you go up to receive your Runners' up medals."

With the camera crew in tow, the journalist jigged over the pitch, heading for Peter's goalkeeper, no doubt wanting to get him to say something that would get the punters clicking their mouse buttons on various sports stories nationwide.

Peter sighed and looked about the stadium where he caught sight of his own fans. Half of the stand, which had been jam-packed ten minutes before, was now empty. Still, a scattering of yellow and blue shirts glinted in the sunshine. His stomach warmed and he summoned up the last of his strength to jog the length of the pitch. When he drew up to them, he held his hands over his head and clapped.

A kid on the front row leant over the advertising hoarding, his cheeks puffed out and eyes red. It tugged at Peter's heartstrings. He swallowed back a mouthful of saliva, yanked the shirt off his back, bundled it up and handed it over to the kid. "Here you go. Might turn out to be quite valuable, that. So hang onto it."

A man drew up alongside the boy in the stand. Presumably the boy's father. He grinned from ear to ear and held up the shirt so that it showed:

Jones 3

"Go on then, Bradley, say thank you," the kid's father said.

The kid brushed away his tears and smiled at Peter. "Thanks."

Peter gave the stand another round of claps, which the fans half-heartedly returned. They knew they had been robbed, too. Just like everyone else in the stadium, they had paid their money and yet Frankston had practically dipped his hands into their pocket and taken it—stolen their day of glory.

The opposing team lined up at the steps, all standing in a line.

Peter's beaten teammates were slumped on the turf beside them, either looking to the ground or up to the heavens. He went over to join them, keeping his distance, not wanting to talk to anybody.

It frightened him that they might see his decision, already made up, in his eyes.

The ceremony passed with the usual melancholy, followed by fanfare.

Once Peter had received his Runners' up medal, he shifted off down the tunnel and into the changing rooms, where he set about getting stripped off and showered.

When he came out, his team mates sat about on the benches, staring at their socked feet. The manager still hadn't put in an appearance, no doubt still giving the officials both barrels over the last minute decision to award the goal. It wouldn't change anything, though.

For right or wrong, they had failed.

2

PETER NEVER allowed his family to attend games.

At the start he had explained it away as some kind of superstition, but in the end he admitted to himself that he was more afraid they'd see him humiliated in some way. If they watched on TV, at least they would be spared the experience first-hand, the supporters' jeers and chants, the embarrassment.

In the end, though, he had just been protecting himself.

When he pulled in through the electric front gate of his house, the light was dimming. Another long summer's evening, when he just wanted today to end and be forgotten.

He hoped the days would show mercy and just skip on by, burying this day in history.

Standing on his own doorstep, he fought back the tears which pricked the corners of his eyes. He just hated to think of the expression on his little girl's face.

What would she think of him, to watch her daddy let her down so publicly?

It was a mercy that she had a day to wait until she had to go to school, face her schoolmates, mostly the boys, and their jokes. He plucked up the courage to ring his doorbell.

His wife, Erica, appeared in the doorway. She had her hair up in a bun, but a few strands dangled down so that they brushed her neck. Her throat bobbed as she swallowed. She brought the door half-closed behind her, as if to afford them a piece of last minute privacy.

Peter managed a half-smile. "I guess you watched on TV."

"Yeah."

"It was a joke, wasn't it?"

"That's what everyone's saying. Talks about it being replayed."

A spark of hope twitched deep in his chest, but he cast it off.

There would be no prospect of that. Logistically, it would be completely impossible. The same old questions about the officials' integrity and the use of technology in the game. It was better just to leave it as it was: yet another ugly stain on football. He shook his head. "I think I'm done."

Lines creased her forehead. She frowned. "What're you talking about?"

"I can't do it anymore. It's a waste of time."

She bowed her head, her chin almost making contact with her chest.

He reached out and held his hand to her neck. She was so sweet and he was letting his world affect everyone else. Football had become just any other job in that respect and he was tired of it.

If there was no honesty in the game then what was the point of going on?

When she looked up, her face was flushed and skin stretched. Her eyes searched his. "Are you sure? It's your life."

"Yeah, this is it."

She nodded then forced a smile. "Better go inside, then."

"I guess."

With a sigh, she pushed back the door and stepped into the hallway. Peter followed her inside, to the sitting room where someone had mercifully turned the TV to some other channel. A film which featured a dog and a boy running about a field. The dog had its tongue lashing in and out of its mouth, while the boy screamed with laughter. His daughter, Rebecca, sat propped up on the arm of the sofa. She turned her head, then rose from her seat. Her replica shirt was untucked from her jeans, hanging down over her curvy waistline. He paced over and embraced her. Her tears dampened his shirt and he felt her hands clamp onto his flanks. "It's not fair," she said.

He placed his hand on the back of her head and stroked her long blond hair. "I know, but that's life."

She drew back and looked at him through her running eyes. "This was different. Everyone saw it, knew what happened. Didn't you see Frankston's celebration? He kissed his hand! Oh you should have seen him in his interview afterwards. He just kept on smiling and joking about it. What an idiot."

A flash of anger passed through Peter, but it was deadened by his overwhelming sensation of defeat. He felt like half the man he'd been that morning. "Nothing we can do."

Her bottom lip wobbled and heavy tears ran down her cheeks.

The sight knotted Peter's insides and he felt heat rise up his own throat. This was the part that he absolutely hated, why he wanted to protect his family from the behemoth of football. But sometimes he was completely impotent.

He embraced her again. "I'm sure there's about a hundred thousand others that feel just like you right now."

Erica entered too and, together, they sat on the sofa in a group hug, the film playing out in the background until night darkened the house and a news programme broke in.

Peter switched it off.

3

PETER'S RETIREMENT sent shockwaves through the football world. A tabloid headline read: Last Giant Calls It Quits, another: End of the Road at Twenty-Eight, and finally: City Captain Throws in the Towel. He read through every article on him, each discussing the various facets and speculating wildly. One claimed he had a gambling problem, which had spiralled out of control, while another believed his daughter had a rare illness and he had made the decision to spend more time with her at this difficult time. None of them carried the argument that he had simply got sick and tired of the game he loved being ruined by cheats.

But, then again, the papers never got anything important right.

Almost everyday someone from the club was on the phone. His manager called up every couple of days, hoping that Peter might change his mind and come back. After all, he was the one who had named Peter captain and so, he assumed, those higher-ups at the club believed Peter owed them something.

Teammates called too, pleading with him to come back, inflating his importance to the dressing room and how they missed him being around. Those lesser-known nicknames floated back to the top: Clown Feet, Skyscraper, Big Dick . . . all somewhat less dignified than the one used by fans and the media:

Giant.

A few weeks passed by and everyone seemed to get the message. Peter's name slipped off the newspaper back pages and his club stopped calling. It was a rare moment of peace in what had otherwise been a hectic life. He remembered it starting when he was about fourteen, when everyone said he had a talent, urged him not to waste it, then it had kicked into a higher gear on signing his first professional contract, with City, at only seventeen.

That had been perhaps the proudest day of his life, at least he recalled all the praise his father had dished out. He'd thought his father might die of pride. Perhaps Peter's enthusiasm for the game had first waned at his father's death, a couple of years ago.

For the first time, he had looked at the fouler parts of the game: the diving, the new generation of divas and showmanship. It was time to call it a day, he was in no doubt now.

He recalled how the joy of his first professional contract had been quickly followed by Erica falling pregnant with Rebecca, and all the worry that'd come with it.

But it'd turned out just fine.

Erica peered around the doorway, into the sitting room, where Peter sat hunched up on the sofa watching a documentary about the Second World War. The dog rested its head on his feet. Erica laid a hand on her hip. "It's two a.m."

"Yeah?"

"Remember what you said to Rebecca this morning?"

His mind whirled back to the conversation. It came back to him. He'd promised that he would go to the school and watch her game. Apparently it was against some local school and held as some kind of local derby. Women's football. He couldn't really abide by it, not that he would say that out loud. It could only do him harm when he was outnumbered two to one in *this* household. Not taking his eyes off the black and white explosions on the screen, he said, "Not really feeling it, to be honest."

Erica strode into the room and stood in front of the TV. The dog stirred in its place, cocking its ears. Now he was for it. Peter looked at Erica, who narrowed her eyes. "Get your arse up off the sofa and go see your little girl play. It's not healthy to sit about the house all day getting fat."

He glanced down at his stomach. Although he hadn't wanted to admit it to himself, he had been putting on the pounds pretty quick. If he wasn't careful, he'd turn into one of those pie-munching, man-mountains which he saw sitting in the stands watching him on a Saturday.

Which he *used* to see.

He lifted himself off the sofa. His body creaked and moaned. The dog yawned and stretched. He looked over at it. *"You're* not getting out of this. Come on."

It bowed its head, arrived at his heel, then followed him out the room.

4

P ETER PARKED UP at the school field. He fumbled through the glove compartment, looking for a pair of sunglasses. Then he checked himself. Over all these years, after all this time slagging off the other footballers for getting to be little dandies and he was threatening to join them. He had to face up to the public, whatever they had to throw at him. What did he care if one of the other parents got a picture of him and sent it off to the local news under some headline like: Giant Looking Rough at Kid's Game.

He got out and the dog jumped to his side.

Together they strolled onto the playing field and across to the football pitch where the girls' team, his daughter somewhere among them, were getting warmed up.

When he reached the touchline, he couldn't resist a quick look about. It wasn't so bad. There was hardly anyone else there at the game. Just a couple of parents over in the corner, about ten or twenty metres from him. He could stay under the radar quite easily.

Then he spotted Rebecca. She wore the number nine shirt and held her hands on her hips, in a way which reminded him of Erica. It sent a warmth through him and made him smile. Another player passed her the ball and she took it in her stride, sending it flying into the top corner of the goal, leaving the goalkeeper no chance. That sent chills through him, but he checked himself.

Surely it had just been a fluke.

He would wait to see how she performed in the game, then he could think about making judgements of her ability.

A referee stepped onto the pitch, a middle-aged man dressed in black.

Peter recognised him as one of the maths teachers from a parents' evening he'd attended a while back. The referee strutted into the centre circle, gave two short, sharp peeps on his whistle and the girls all got into their formations.

Peter's gaze remained on Rebecca, standing on the edge, completely focussed. He considered giving her a wave, letting her know that he was there, supporting her, but he recognised the look on her face—solid determination.

That was the same look he had seen in the mirror.

The game got underway and the players jostled for possession. For most of the first half, the opposition dominated and, a few minutes before halftime, they scored.

Peter caught Rebecca's eye as she walked back to the semi-circle for the restart. It was almost as if she didn't recognise him, her expression remaining neutral, completely driven and focussed. The game went on in the same vein and the referee blew for halftime. The two teams crowded about their respective managers.

Something twitched in Peter's gut, a feeling it had been a long time since he had felt.

That hunger and pride, the risk of the game.

More than anything he wanted to get involved.

Before he knew it, he was striding across the field, the dog at his heel. When he arrived at the group, being shepherded by a female PE teacher, who Peter was sure he'd never met, they all turned their heads to him.

Peter was used to people pointing and staring. In the street, in the supermarket, anywhere he went people would turn their heads and mutter. However, in this case, it only worked to his advantage. He had the entire group's attention. So, instead of thinking about the moment, he got down to business and stepped into the middle of the group.

The dog sat and craned its neck up, watching on with the rest.

Peter clapped his hands. "That wasn't a bad first half, but I'd like to see a bit more bite. Chase them down more. Play the simple passes. You're surrendering the ball too much." He pointed at the girl he'd noticed playing in central midfield. "You need to get back and help out your defenders, otherwise they'll run riot. Same in attack, you need to get it forward. I don't want to see you walk one metre in the second half."

The girl turned white but nodded along.

Peter turned to Rebecca, warding off a slight tingle in his gut. There was no sign of embarrassment or horror on her face—she was listening to his every word, like the others. "You need to drop back and help out the midfield. It's doing no one any good with you lingering about miles away from the ball." He clapped again. "All right, go out there and get a result." He returned to his place on the touchline, allowing the dog to nuzzle his hand.

The team came out with added *bite* in the second half and the girls worked much harder, running to close down. Peter knew what he saw in their faces. It was a mixture of fear and determination. They didn't want to let him down. That feeling that a group of people were trying their best to impress him made him happier than anything else. It was like he was back at City, with his teammates working hard for him.

With fifteen minutes to go, the game remained at one-nil. Although Rebecca's team had had a few chances, the finishing had been woeful. Now, however, the central midfielder, who Peter had spoken to at halftime, got the ball just inside the opponents' half and pinged it into the box, where Rebecca controlled it with her first touch and, with her second, slipped it into the bottom corner of the net.

Peter's stomach dropped and he punched the air in celebration. The girls all crowded around, patting each other on the back, then they jogged back to the halfway line.

Peter couldn't prevent the smile breaking out on his face. He was sure that Rebecca really had something.

The game ticked away and Rebecca's team got a corner in the last minute. Rebecca strode up to take it. Peter wanted to shout out, to tell her to let someone else cross the ball so that she would be in the box, but he kept his mouth shut.

Rebecca fired in a swinging cross which found the head of one of the defenders. It flew right into the top corner of the net and the referee blew for fulltime.

They had won the game.

Lightning tickled his chest, but he kept a lid on it. He had never in his wildest dreams thought his daughter might be as talented as this.

The girls shook hands with the opposition then made their way about the warm down. Once again, the female PE teacher gave them the orders. Then she caught Peter's eye and strode toward him. Peter thought she might be about to give him a dressing down, for running onto the pitch. In retrospect he had been a bit of a twat. She drew up to him, holding out her hand for him to shake. He accepted it, and she said, "Haven't seen you around here before."

"No, I've usually had training or match preparation when Rebecca's had a game."

"I see."

He nodded to the group of girls. "She's quite good, isn't she?"

She smiled. "Seems to take after her dad in that way."

"I hope not."

The PE teacher glanced across the group of girls then looked back in his eye. "What're you up to at the moment?"

"What do you mean?"

"Well, since you've called time on your playing career, have you thought of coming down here and giving the girls some coaching."

The idea seemed quite absurd. He had just got out of the game and it was already sucking him back in. With a click of his fingers, he brought the dog to his side. "Not sure about that." He smiled and headed off toward the car park. "Nice to meet you, anyway."

"Give it some thought, please, Mr Jones."

5

ON THE DRIVE back home, like normal, Peter couldn't think of anything to talk about with Rebecca. So, like he always did whenever in doubt about something, he decided to talk about football.

He led her through his analysis of her strengths and weaknesses, where she needed to improve her skills. Then, once that conversation had died a death, he brought up the PE teacher's comments to lighten the mood. He shifted up to third and swooped around the corner, out of town and into the country. "You won't guess what your coach said after the game."

"What?"

"She wanted me to get involved with the girls' team. Give you some tips."

Rebecca looked out the window, her eyes darting about the blurred landscapes. The dog slept in her floor space, resting its head on her knee. "Doesn't sound like too bad of a plan."

Something twitched in his chest. He had been expecting laughter, but she was giving him a proper hearing. Now he would have to go about defending why he shouldn't accept. He swallowed. They came to a long, flat stretch and he moved up to fourth. "I don't know. It just doesn't seem right for me to get involved. I'd bring too much baggage."

"What do you mean?"

His chest tightened and he kept his eyes on the road a few seconds, hoping that the question might just disintegrate into thin air. But he knew he had to give her an answer. "I've just got out of the game and I'm not sure I enjoy it anymore."

"Don't think I didn't catch you smiling watching me play. I saw it on your face."

He nodded and steered the car about the familiar village,

pausing when he reached their electric gate, which he opened with the fob. He parked up outside the garage door and turned off the ignition.

She turned to him, her eyes taking on a watery quality. Her strong voice gave way a little. "What do you say then, Dad?"

What could he say to that? He shifted in his seat, attempting to avoid her gaze, but he knew it was impossible.

So, he just nodded.

With a squeal, she leapt across the handbrake and wrapped her arms about his neck. Her grip didn't let off for a long time. He sat where he was, thinking about whether he was doing the right thing. When he looked over at the dog, at Rebecca's feet, it was staring at him with its tongue flicking in and out of its mouth, as if it was pleased that he'd accepted the offer too.

6

THE SCHOOL put Peter onto the official coaching staff for the girls' football team. He had a conversation with the head teacher, who tried to convince him he really might be better used on the *boys'* team. Then he had to sign up for coaching courses in the evenings, with a bunch of Year Elevens. He had never thought about all the ins and outs, the paperwork, he'd have to get done just to coach his daughter. But he supposed it was all for the best.

Once everything was finished, he set about preparing the training sessions.

To begin with, he and the PE teacher made for an uncomfortable dynamic.

The PE teacher would illustrate some point which would lead to Peter interrupting with some 'real world' advice and he would set the girls right. In the end, it was just Peter taking the entire coaching session, while the PE teacher watched on from the side lines. When he had got his coaching badge, the PE teacher stopped coming altogether—probably glad to have her evenings free from then on.

In the class there were huge gaps in ability. If he had been put under pressure, he would've picked out the goalkeeper, Janet, the central midfielder, Helen, and, of course, Rebecca as being a notch above the rest.

It was enough to build a team, in any case.

When they played practice matches, he got the girls to keep those three players in mind and, before long, they got the idea that if they wanted to win, more often than not, they had to get the ball to them.

After a few months, kids stopped coming up to him and asking for autographs. Indeed, even out and about in town, people didn't bother him so much. It seemed that the football world had moved on since his retirement.

He didn't even check the scores anymore.

The girls' football calendar was mostly made up of a local league with a few friendlies sprinkled about. However, what interested Peter the most was the cup coming up in a couple of weeks. He knew that a decent cup run could easily lift the spirits of a team and lead to better results elsewhere.

That was where he would concentrate his motivation efforts.

In any case, the football was almost secondary to his blossoming relationship with his daughter. At the end of that day's training, they headed back home, pulling up to the house both wearing wide smiles. When they poured in through the door, Erica had a frown on her face, which immediately had a sobering effect on Peter. It made him feel guilty. Erica embraced Rebecca, who then headed upstairs, her kitbag hanging off her shoulder. Once she was out of sight, Peter knew he was for it. Eric crossed her arms and spoke in a hushed voice. "I just got a phone call from one of the parents."

Wanting to deflect as much of this attack as possible, he bent down and ruffled the dog's ears. "Really?"

"Yes, she was worried about her daughter being around a male football coach."

He snorted. "You can't be serious."

"They sounded very serious."

He straightened. "What're they saying I've done?"

"Nothing, from what I can gather. It just seems like they don't like the idea."

"Do I look like a kiddie-fiddler to you?"

"No."

"I've been with the PE teacher during most of the sessions. Only this week I've started training with them alone."

"I know."

The whole situation had taken him aback somewhat. Things were going really well with the girls. They were all eleven or twelve, for God's sake, who could even think of them like that?

If he hadn't been wholly committed to the team, coaching them to some form of success, he was now. There was no way some mother who read too many tabloids was going to ruin his new-found relationship with his daughter.

He yawned and padded into the sitting room, where he flicked on the TV.

Erica sighed and headed into the kitchen. "Dinner's on the table in ten minutes. Don't get too comfy."

7

THE CUP GAME approached fast. As each day passed by, Peter got more and more nervous, although he kept his constant smile and continued to dish out his words of encouragement. Now he made a point of keeping his distance from the girls, not wanting to give anyone evidence to use against him. His own daughter was part of the team, did they really think he was not only sick enough to do something with these children, but with his own daughter?

It turned his guts inside out just imagining it.

After the training session, he brought all the girls together in a huddle. Over their heads and shoulders, he made out the waiting parents, all at their cars, standing about chatting among themselves.

He wondered about the gossip.

Could they really be talking about him?

Planning out ways that they could get him away from their girls?

It was better just to put it out of his mind and keep his brain concentrated on the task at hand. He clapped his hands together and put on his captain's face. "Brilliant stuff today, girls, just what I was looking for. Think we'll give them a real game on Saturday. Remember your individual drills and try your best to get them in everyday up until the game. Use your back garden, go to a local park, wherever you can find a bit of space to get it done." His eyes fell on a mother in the crowd who stared at him intently. "All right, then, have a good evening."

The girls skipped off in groups, chattering. Some headed over to their waiting parents, while others got a few more minutes playing in the goal, taking turns shooting and goalkeeping. All this enthusiasm warmed Peter's heart, took him back to his own days —before he'd turned pro.

Now he knew *that* had been the golden part of his life.

The mother who had been staring at him paced across the turf, her head bowed and arms pumping. Peter thought about grabbing Rebecca and making a run for the car park. He didn't like these parent-coach conferences. It always ended up with him having to give them some encouraging comment about their offspring.

And now there was this gossip hanging over his head.

He just wanted to get home, get on the sofa with the dog and a beer in hand.

The mother drew up to him and smiled. "You must be Peter Jones."

"That's right."

"My husband knows all about you from the football. I've never been much of a fan myself, so I wouldn't know."

"Your daughter's in the team."

Her eyes ran across the girls having a kick about in the goal mouth. "Yes, I'm Helen's mum."

"Right."

Still watching the girls, she pressed her lips together and cocked her head. "Mr Jones, I've been talking with a few of the girls' parents and they've expressed a few concerns about you taking their sessions."

His heart beat faster. He glanced about, trying to pick out Rebecca in case he had to flee a group of manic parents. He took a deep breath. "I see."

"Yes, it's just a little odd having a male coach for the girls' team, don't you think? I mean, wouldn't you be better used in the boys' team?"

"My *daughter's* in the team."

This seemed to catch the mother off guard. She pulled back. "Oh, is she?"

"Yeah, Rebecca."

The mother considered this a few moments, shot a glance over at the other parents, then looked back at Peter. "That aside, we do feel that it would be more appropriate to put Miss Yemons back in charge of the team. It's a very sensitive time for these girls, lots of changes, and I think she acted as a kind of confidant in many ways."

Peter met Rebecca's eye as she drew back from the penalty box, lining up a shot. Then he glanced at the mother. "Well, I have to tell you that I shared the responsibility with Miss Yemons for the first few weeks, and I don't remember much of the sort. I think we both maintain the same distance between the girls and ourselves."

That seemed to have ripped through her argument somewhat, but she kept her chin raised, determined not to be defeated so easily. "We'd just feel better about it."

Peter wanted to tell her that life wasn't like everything she read in the tabloids, but he held back. In these sensitive situations it paid off to be more diplomatic. He would make a deal. That gave people a greater sense of control. He nodded at the girls. "Tell you what. How about we wait until the cup game on Saturday. If we lose then I'll have no qualms about stepping aside. But I really think we've made great progress so far."

"I have to say that our daughters' performances are something of a secondary issue. Their safety should be put first."

"Even so, let's leave it till Saturday. Then you can judge me a bit better. See that I have been putting a shift in with these girls."

The mother shrunk back, shot one of the other parents at the car park a look, then nodded and moved off. Peter allowed himself to breathe again. His eyes traced the girls who continued to play in the penalty area, kicking the ball between themselves.

Then he caught Rebecca's face in his gaze.

For the sake of their relationship, he hoped they could stay together.

8

S ATURDAY ROLLED AROUND and Peter went about getting everything ready, in real haste.

The house resembled something of a pre-ceremony panic. Rebecca rushed about with various pieces of football kit in her arms, while Erica darted back and forth organising something in the kitchen, or turning some appliance off or on. Peter stood at the door and waited, the dog sitting at his side, its ears perked and eyes following each new bustle.

Finally, they piled into the car and headed for the playing field.

Mist still hung in the air and dew turned the grass damp and silver. Several parents and their daughters had already shown up. Younger brothers and sisters played about in the nets, some swinging from the posts. One girl had managed to get herself on top of the bar, where she sat and watched over everyone with a smug look.

Peter chased them all off and laid out fluorescent orange cones for the warm up. He noticed the parents staring on from the side lines, mums and dads, all of them apparently uncomfortable about him being there, helping their daughters.

About ten minutes later, the opposing team showed up.

The group of girls poured out of the van, led by a robust middle-aged woman who held a football at her chest. When she looked about, her features screwed up, as if she were somewhat embarrassed about having to play at this field. She strolled up to Peter and held out her hand. "Suppose that you're the coach, then?"

"That's right."

She shot another glance across the field. "Ground looks a bit mushy for my taste."

"Can't help that. The grounds men have done their best."

"Might send off a complaint to the local authority. Get the match replayed at ours."

A shred of fear tore through Peter.

After all the anxiety and pressure he'd built up around this game, the promise he'd made with one of the mothers based on today's result, he couldn't afford to let it slip away from him. He eyed the woman through the corner of his eye. "Seems a lot of bother. I'm sure it'll be fine for us."

She dropped the ball to the ground and trapped it under her right foot. Then she turned over her hand, inspected her nails and headed off to the other end of the pitch. "If one of my players picks up an injury here, there'll be hell to pay."

In his mind, Peter swore at her. This was some kind of mind game she was playing on him, trying to make it seem like they were lucky to be given the privilege of playing their team. He wouldn't stand for it, not let it affect his team. After he'd brought all his players together for a team talk, he sent them out onto the field to get the job done.

At halftime Peter's team were three-nil up. Two for Rebecca. He caught a glance at the opposing coach's face. Her features were all creased up and she looked as if she were ready to rip off someone's head. Still, she could have no complaints. The surface hadn't held any surprises, for either team.

He had beaten her.

The second half went along the same route and they ended the game winning five-nil. The opposing team held out their shaking hands and headed off to their team mini-bus with their heads bowed. When Peter attempted to shake the opposing coach's hand, she simply stormed off after her girls. Cup games were difficult. Qualification or elimination. All or nothing. He resisted the temptation to sneer, too overjoyed to allow negative emotions to seep into his body.

Rebecca trotted up and threw her arms about him. The dog

followed with Erica soon after. He savoured her warm embrace, while catching the mother he'd spoken to a few days earlier over their shoulders. Her face was like fire and he would need to confront her before too long, but at least he had been granted a stay of execution.

People dribbled away from the playing field, leaving only Peter and his family, standing there alone. Now it was just a question of what to do for the rest of the free Saturday.

9

THE WEEKS PASSED BY and Peter continued to coach the girls' team. However he did feel the strain of parents eyes constantly on his back: the occasional overheard remark or well-chosen silence. So, it wasn't with an awful amount of surprise that he was summoned by the Parent Teacher Association.

On the evening of the meeting, he concentrated on getting himself ready, putting on a shirt and tie—feeling like a right dweeb.

He gave Erica a kiss then bounded out the door and drove to the school.

Parents already sat about the hall, chatting amongst themselves. He slunk in and took up an aisle seat several rows back from the front. Inside his chest, he held some vague hope they might just forget about him. However this was put to rest when the mother, the one who'd spoken to him, entered the hall and gestured for him to sit up front, in one of the six plastic chairs laid out to face the audience. While they waited, they didn't say a word. About five minutes later, the crowd was filled and the mother stood up to talk. She led the meeting through various topics before coming to the issue of the girls' team coach.

There were several rustles and whispers amongst the audience.

"If I could just have a bit of quiet." She raised her hand and the conversations spluttered out. "Now, we've been very lucky for Mr Jones, here, to offer his coaching expertise for the girls' football teams. However, there have been a number of parents who have expressed concern about having a male coach taking this partic-ular extra-curricular activity."

Some more murmuring amongst the audience.

Peter smoothed his tie and looked down at his well-polished shoes.

Brown, the plainest ones he had.

A man at the back stood up and raised his hand. "Did well on Saturday, though, winning five-nil."

The mother cocked her head and smiled. "While that's true, I believe some hold other, more *pressing*, concerns."

"Like what? Being afraid of the school having a bit of success for once?"

A round of chuckles was brought swiftly under control by the mother. "We must remember that the girls' team features children who are between eleven and twelve years old. It is a sensitive time and they should perhaps have someone more in-tune to their concerns."

There was no way that Peter could keep himself out of this now. He had to get in his own view. He raised his hand, but the mother either didn't see him or ignored him.

"What I propose is to re-instate Miss Yemons as the coach."

Somewhere at the back of the hall there was a groan. Peter was glad to see that Miss Yemons wasn't in the hall that night. It might've made for an awkward situation. Then again, he saw these people had no qualms doing someone down when they had numbers.

Here they were talking about him like he was some kind of paedophile.

Another man stood up. "Listen, maybe you don't know much about football, but Giant Jonesy here is the best thing that ever happened to City. Now, maybe I don't completely agree with his retirement, but I think we should take all he's got to offer before he comes to his senses."

The crowd roared.

It stirred something deep inside Peter, reminding him of the crowd on those Saturday matches, the three o'clock kick offs—like some kind of shadow of that buzz. His confidence grew and he stood, not taking any notice of the mother who was glaring holes in his skull. "What some of you might not realise is that my daughter's in the team." He held up his palms. "I'm not saying that's a reason for you to trust your girls to me, but I'm telling you straight out now that my only intention is to refind my passion for the game. I believe a lot of these girls have the talent to take this sport further"—by 'a lot' he meant Janet, Helen and Rebecca—"and I'd like to see where this cup run gets us. Like I told this lady a few days back, as soon as things go pear-shaped, I'll be prepared to walk away." He sat back down, content that he'd said his piece.

The mother stood up in the stunned silence of the hall. She brushed back a loose strand of hair, tucking it behind her ear. "Well, I suppose the only reasonable way to resolve this situation is with a vote. So, all those in favour of reinstating Miss Yemons?"

Half a dozen hands rose.

She paused a few seconds, not doubt hoping a landslide of opinion might hit, but it remained the minority. "And keeping Mr Jones?"

Almost the entire hall raised their hands.

The mother looked perplexed then bent down, snatching up the sheet and reading off the next point for discussion.

When the drinks break rolled around, Peter snuck out and drove back home.

10

P ETER KEPT UP the same job, knowing that the majority of parents were behind him. That made things much easier. From now on he didn't have to look back over his shoulder, constantly worrying about what people were saying.

The team slipped through the next few cup games without much trouble. His techniques put the girls miles ahead of their opposition, so much so that he felt bad about it, thought that he might be cheating in some way. But, in the end, he contented himself with the fact that this was part of his therapy. Already he was feeling better about the game, more attuned to it. In the end, the team got through to the final. That evening he got an email from the local authority, with the information for the venue.

It was to be held at City's ground.

A shiver ran down his spine and he looked over the information again, sure that he might've got it wrong. But there it was, in black and white. The date and time all stamped.

Could he do it, return there?

He would have to buckle up and take it on the chin.

There was no way he would let the girls down now.

Not when they had all the momentum.

The day of the final arrived and they set off for the City ground, Peter already feeling his body shot to pieces from nerves. They parked up then headed through the all-too familiar gates where the pitch was all laid out, crisp and ready for the afternoon's game. The stands stood empty, and would hardly fill up much for a school girls' match. Nonetheless, he read the excitement on Rebecca's face. He'd half-expected her to tell him not to come today, some kind of revenge at him never letting his family come to the games.

With all the match preparation done, he sent the girls out onto the field to kick off, taking up his own seat in the stand beside Erica. They had come this far and it was down to them now.

A few minutes after kick off, he felt a tap on his shoulder.

He looked around to see a familiar-looking woman, about his age, in her late-twenties, early-thirties. Often he had noticed her drifting about the club but, was ashamed to admit, that he had never quite understood her function. She raised her eyebrows. "We were having bets to see if you were going to turn up today."

"Really? This has nothing to do with me. It's about the girls. Their day to enjoy."

She squinted and pointed at the pitch. "It's Rebecca, that's your girl, isn't it?"

"That's right."

"I'll be keeping an eye on her today, but I've been to see her before. We're definitely interested in her development."

Then the penny dropped.

He remembered catching the woman walking about the club with a name badge.

She was the manager of City's female team. His heart itched. He tried to think about what to say. His first instinct was to protect his daughter, but he knew that this might well be an excellent offer—if she performed today.

Sure, there wasn't much money in women's football . . . yet.

Then again, wasn't that what had got him involved in the girls' team in the first place, it being a purer form of the game?

He scanned the pitch, wondering whether Rebecca had thought of the prospect of City signing her. Having coached and watched her over the last few weeks, he was convinced that she had talent.

The referee blew for the kick off and the game started. Players jostled for position and many passes went astray. It wasn't a fluid match and Peter noticed the woman behind him shifting in her seat. He thought she might get up and leave at any second. It made him wonder whether he would care at all, whether it would be better for Rebecca to stay like this forever.

At halftime, the match stayed at nil-nil.

Peter got up and went down to give his team talk. When he had wrapped it up, Rebecca stayed behind from the other girls. She glanced up into the stand. "I know who that is, sitting behind you."

"You do?"

"It's Stacey Harrison."

It was a little embarrassing that Rebecca knew more about a part of City than he did. He resisted the urge to turn and look, not wanting Stacey to know that they were talking about her. "Just concentrate on your performance and the result will come."

Blood drained from Rebecca's cheeks and her eyes widened. "You don't think she's judging us today, do you? I mean, this won't be the only chance I'll get, will it?"

He rested his hand on her shoulder. "I shouldn't think so. Just relax out there. Enjoy it. That's all I ask."

When she turned back and headed toward the pitch, her shoulders were slumped and she kept away from the other girls. Peter returned to his seat, giving Stacey a polite nod. Every couple of seconds, she looked back at the stand. Erica waved to her, believing she was looking for family support.

Toward the end of the second half, the opposing team scored. Peter knew, at the back of his mind, that Rebecca's team didn't have the strength to score a goal. They looked wet behind the ears and had been seen off by an experienced unit. When the referee whistled for fulltime, Peter set off back down to pitch side, where he consoled the girls.

Some were in tears.

The mother, who had wanted him away from coaching the team, drew up alongside him, her eyebrows arched. "I suppose that's the end of your run, too, then?"

Peter had thought he might feel some resentment to her, but he sucked it up and remained calm. This did feel like the ending of something. "Seems so."

She nodded and disappeared.

He wrapped his arms about Rebecca, who had her head bowed and tears streaming down her cheeks. Her body was warm and her arms drew about him like vines. "It's not so bad," he said, "you did fine out there. Just got beaten by a better team."

Through her muted sobs, she muttered, "It's all ruined."

It jangled his heartstrings. He wanted to tell her that enjoying the game was what mattered, not always taking it to another level. But he knew that those words were useless for someone, like him, who had just suffered defeat. So he only squeezed her and made sympathetic noises. Erica arrived and took up her other side and between them they made their way toward the car park.

"Wait a moment."

A shrill voice, which Peter immediately recognised as belonging to Stacey. He looked back. Had she come to offer her own condolences?

There was nothing more useless than the sympathy of a stranger.

She was grinning ear-to-ear and panting from her run. "Thought I'd missed you there. Didn't want to interrupt the moment." She looked to Rebecca. "We'd like to offer you a youth contract."

Peter's mind melted and his pulse rattled his veins.

Rebecca prised herself away from her parents. She rubbed tears from her cheeks. "Really?"

"Yes. Helen and Janet, too. Training twice a week. Matches on Sunday mornings. What do you say?"

Rebecca turned and looked to her parents, as if asking permission.

Peter looked deep into her eyes and shrugged. "It's completely up to you."

Without a second's pause, Rebecca beamed at Stacey. "Yes, *yes*!"

"That's great," Stacey said, then headed off, with a wave. "Be here on Wednesday at six where you can meet your teammates."

They all stood about, like pillars.

Rebecca looped her arm through Peter's. "You're really sure about this, Dad? It doesn't go against anything you believe in?"

"No, I don't think so. You'll do great, do us proud, I reckon."

"And you won't have second thoughts about going back to playing?"

A glimmer of hope lit in his chest, dwindled, then expired.

There wasn't any point.

For now money wasn't an issue, but he might find a way back in with coaching.

That seemed the future now.

He shook his head. "I'm done. Lost my faith. But I'm sure you'll play for the both of us."

YOU ARE NOT GLADIATORS

1

P UFFIN sat up in his articulated chair, a cat on his lap, one on the feet, and another all stretched out on his shoulders. All three of them purring away. All of three of them oblivious to the kerfuffle going on outside.

Right outside the front door.

Out in the street.

Puffin wore his thick—fleecy—burgundy-tone dressing grown, all done up tight to the brink of his neck. His initials PW: Puffin Willoughby, were etched out in gold thread over the left breast pocket. The garment as a whole made him feel quite grand indeed.

He also had tartan blankets tucked in up from his knees to his chest, to keep the draught out.

Heating this time of year was a waste of money, or at least that was what he used to tell his wife . . . before she'd died.

And he didn't hear an awful lot of complaining now.

But, all things considered, he was comfortable as he sat at his mahogany writing desk, with his florid-tipped fountain pen and made the scratches on the draft copy of what would finally become his will.

And nobody was getting anything.

That was the crux of the matter.

Though it took some mighty elaborate wording and some knotted-up thinking to make it so that some snub-nosed, cheap-suited lawyer wouldn't try and find a loophole in it.

He wrestled the arms of his glasses out from behind his ears, reached out for his mug of cocoa, and then discovered that he'd already drained it.

Fine, that was just fine.

The last time he'd been checked over by a doctor—what was it, like five or six years ago now, when they'd somehow collared him in a shopping centre . . . some bone-witted, *meathead* had seen his way to saying that Puffin had looked 'red in the face' . . . and that had brought the doctor scurrying out of the woodwork . . . *just* like a woodlouse.

Or a termite.

Depending on how Puffin's mood lay with him that particular day of reflection.

Or night, seeing as, by the hands of the crystal-windowed carriage clock which ticked away on the desk, it was a little after three in the morning.

Far, *far* too late . . . or too early? . . . to be out and making a racket in the street.

Though, if he'd had it his way, no one would *ever* be allowed to make anything above a whisper out in the street.

Often, when he'd fantasised about himself being prime minister, he had wondered just how soon it would take a citizens' protest to toss him from power.

. . . But what had it been about the doctor, and the cocoa, and the . . . the *shopping* centre.

Yes, that was right, the doctor had taken his blood pressure, and told him to *cut back* on sugars, and glutton, and . . . a whole cascade of other things that he had *no* intention whatsoever of *ever* cutting back on.

He *so* loved the smell of cocoa, if not the taste. That thick, and sweet, and smooth, and silky taste of chocolate . . . and when he prepared it—as he always did—with milk . . . why it was enough to make a grown man weep.

. . . If Puffin had *ever* been the crying kind. Which he most certainly never had.

There was another round of bellowing out in the street.

Clapping.

Rowdy shouting.

Egging one another on.

Puffin thought of the other residents of Limshore Close, why there was Mrs Weaver, and there was Mrs Gurnica, and there was . . . well, a whole flock of woolly-haired widows, and then there was he, the only widower on the whole *damn* street.

And, no doubt, the one who bore the responsibility of sorting out this whole *damn* mess with this group of adolescents—or where they young *adults?*—scarpering about making ordinary folk's sleep a non-existent misery.

Though, truth told, as Puffin turned it over, he couldn't think of a single one of his friends—*God*, that was *such* an inaccurate term, since the only thing uniting them was their mutual generational lapse into agedness—who could sleep through the night any longer.

Of the ones who told the truth, in any case.

And not many of them did.

But he *knew* the truth, without them even having to say it. Because, like them—*just* like them—he was a fighter, the one who had *survived*.

At least just so that he might die alone, and at peace, and at home.

So, with a *creaking* of the bones, and the protesting of the muscles, and the mewling of the cats brought round from their naps—or were they *really* in deep *cat* sleep?—he prised himself up and into his lambswool-lined slippers and trudged through the darkened house, the only light, in fact, the desk lamp that he was leaving behind.

That was for the best.

If there was one thing he had learned from his seventy-three years of life, it was that darkness was the greatest friend to surprise.

Surprises *always* seemed to leap right out of the dark.

Right when you were least expecting it.

When he reached the front door, Puffin paused, held up his

hand to look out through the frosted glass there to try and determine just what was going on out in the street.

Strange. All was quiet. Not a stirring.

The glass was cool against his mottled, fish-skin flesh. And that pleasant taste of the cocoa from before had been replaced by an odd, almost bloody taste. He breathed in the glass deeply, taking in its neutral smell, and trying to displace that bitter taste.

He listened a little harder.

Perhaps the boys had taken their leave. Gone off to their teenage bedrooms . . . or were they older? . . . goodness, with every year it got harder and harder to tell ages of the younger generations, not because of the way that young faces had a habit of constantly changing, at least that wasn't true in Puffin's case, but it had more to do with the fact that really, deeply, and sincerely, Puffin just couldn't care less about *anyone* else in the world.

Hence the will. And making well and truly *sure* that there was no way of any*one* getting any*thing* out of him. He swore to himself that he would literally turn in his grave if anyone did manage it.

And find some way, *anyway*, to bite them.

Yes, that was right, *bite* them.

Puffin turned his attention back to the street outside. He couldn't *hear* any more of a racket going on out there. Might it be possible the boys had actually all moved on?

He was on the brink of turning around, of shipping back off to his comfortable armchair, with his trio of cats all waking, when he heard, quite distinct, and rippling through the air almost with the same abruptness and volume of a siren, a great and unshakable, *"Wahay!"*

For a septuagenarian, Puffin sure could pummel a front-door latch when he needed to.

And right now he really needed to.

He pounded it down, released the catch, and stood on his doorstep, staring out into the streetlamp-lit street.

2

TWELVE OF THEM.

Puffin didn't need his glasses to count them.

Big ones, little ones, ginger ones, black-haired ones, all different tones of skin, it seemed, and every one different from the next.

This racial variation wasn't what caught Puffin's attention, though. Oh no. It was the fact that all of them—all *twelve* of them— were dressed in bed sheets.

White bed sheets.

Togas? Was that the idea?

And some wore leather-strapped sandals, while others were in flip flops. A few of them were simply in bare feet, apparently not bothered about running about cutting up their feet on glass and much worse.

Had Puffin stumbled back in time, not only tripped out of his country of birth, but gone through some sort of time vortex?

No, of course that wasn't the answer.

The answer was far more plain.

Much more obvious.

In the dewy morning air he could smell that sour scent of beer . . . *lager* . . . following these boys about.

Lager, lager, lager, and who knew what else?

Because that was all he could smell.

He supposed, considering this lewd behaviour these boys were getting up to, they might've been drinking something a little heavier.

Whisky? Or vodka?

. . . Did people—*young* people—still drink gin?

That was so much unrequired information.

He wondered whether he should call the police . . . though he rejected it almost instantly, out of hand, because, as he had declared long ago, the day that he called up the *police* to come fight his battles for him would be the day that he was ready for them to slip him in the hole, on those elastic baggage straps, and allow the worms to commence their feasting.

Nope. There would be no police.

Just polite, reasoned argument.

Or, as polite and reasoned as Puffin could make it.

Puffin cleared his throat and set foot on his garden path. He listened to the faint *crunch* of gravel, almost muted against the sounds of those boys' caterwauling.

Sure enough, as Puffin reached his garden gate, the rickety metal monstrosity that he'd always intended to replace, but never bothered to do so . . . his wife had often nagged him about fitting a nice, prim, white-washed wooden gate there, and he supposed that once she'd copped it, he'd just never really given it much thought.

And he wouldn't give it any more right now.

The boys were all clustered about a streetlamp. Their backs to Puffin as he approached. They chittered and chatted, all their shoulders trembling with laughter. And they all seemed to be looking down. Looking down to the centre of the group.

To someone between them.

As Puffin drew closer, his breath came out between his lips in a fine mist, and he could feel the cold, raw bite of the northern wind as it blew down the street.

In a way, he was quite looking forward to this.

He *did* truly enjoy giving the *yoof* a proper talking to now and again.

One of his true pleasures, in fact.

About five paces off those turned backs, Puffin cleared his throat and said, "Excuse me?"

They all kept their backs to him. Not one of them bothering to turn round to so much as mutter a swearword or deliver a wad of spit.

A total blank.

So Puffin did what was only reasonable, and he raised his voice. "Excuse me!"

One of them turned round. A boy with a black face, and light-brown eyes. A squat, plump nose, and a plumper chin. "Wha'?"

Puffin settled in a little, tried to get a glance around the boy, to whatever it was that they were concentrating on down there at their feet . . . in the centre of the circle.

But he couldn't get so much as a glimpse.

He turned his attention back to the boy who had provided him with an entry into discourse. "You do realise that this is a residential street? That people here are trying to get a good night's rest?"

Another boy turned back from the group. This one was flame-haired and had freckles.

Something about gingers had always rubbed Puffin up the wrong way. He had no idea why. Perhaps some childhood trauma. Maybe some redhead doctor had jabbed him with a needle or pinched him behind his mother's back.

Puffin had never been all that interested in psychoanalysis, if that was truly the name for it.

"Wha' you wan'?" the ginger boy said.

"Oh," Puffin said, raising his eyebrows a little. "What I'd *like* is for you and your friends to go scarper off somewhere else to play."

"Wha's Granddad up to, eh?" another boy said, beside the ginger boy, a *black*-haired boy.

Puffin had no particular feelings, either for or against black-haired people, since he had been one himself . . . before his hair had given up the fight and turned white on him . . . and then fallen out altogether, save for a few random wisps here and there.

Puffin had no intention of repeating himself. He'd made his

wishes perfectly clear. And now was the time for the boys to deliver their response.

So he waited.

And waited.

He watched the black-haired boy nudge another boy in the ribs, and then, soon enough, they were all chatting among themselves, casting the odd glance in Puffin's direction.

Puffin kept his expression neutral. *Reasonable.* If there was anything he'd learned in the course of his life, it was that when dealing with drunks it was incredibly important not to rile them in anyway.

Or if you did wish to jibe them a little, it was important to do it in such a way that they couldn't understand.

After another series of hurried whispers, the boys cast glances at Puffin, before dipping their heads into the circle.

Puffin wondered, once again, just how far adrift he was of the world now. It truly was as if the whole place had simply grown legs and moved off.

These things . . . *things* young people did.

They just seemed so *alien* and so *illogical.*

As one, the boys all spun round, faced up to Puffin and yelled, at the tops of their voices, "This! Is! Sparta!" and, again as one, they ran towards Puffin.

And then around him.

And he watched them, their bed sheets still clinging to their drunken frames, as they disappeared off around the corner, and into the night.

Off to go annoy someone else.

Thank *God.*

And Puffin, too, was on the point of moving off, off heading back to his house, and getting on with the writing of the will, when he noticed, out of the corner of his eye, that there was still one boy remaining.

He sat on the pavement, back pressed up against the streetlamp.

A couple of seconds later, Puffin realised that the boy had his hands tied behind his back. That the boy was *tied* to the streetlamp. And his friends had simply left him here.

This boy had a bird nest of brown hair, which Puffin had learned to associate with accountants, and bank assistants and people who generally didn't like getting their hands dirty. Dependable. Unshakable people.

And perhaps it was that sentiment, at least at work *subconsciously* which drew Puffin to *not* turn around and return to his dozing cats, and the unfinished will.

This boy, quite simply put, was a fish out of water.

As Puffin approached the boy, he noticed the flourish of a curtain. Up in the bedroom of a house overlooking the street.

Mrs Weaver.

He looked over this boy again. Saw his youthful face. And the way the other boys had bound his hands behind his back using a battered and frayed-looking, blue rope.

But it seemed to do the trick.

Not letting the boy move from the spot.

The *patter* of footsteps faded off in the distance as the other boys all disappeared into the night. Their chuckling also faded away. But that stink of lager still wafted up in the air, apparently unkillable.

"Are you all right there?" Puffin said.

The boy slowly tilted his head up. His eyes were all groggy, cheeks all puffed up and red, and his lips slightly parted. ". . . Yeah, fine, thanks," the boy said after a little while.

"You, uh, do not look *all right.*"

"I am, thank you."

Puffin made fists of his hands and rested the knuckles against the waistband of his dressing gown. "What, ah, is all this about then?"

"Is wha' abou'?"

"You know," Puffin said, flapping his hands at the boy to indicate his getup, "the bed sheets. What's that all about?"

"Oh," the boy said, looking away from Puffin, and down at his bare feet. "Well, you see, we're all dressed up as gladiators."

Puffin thought this over for a moment. Wondered whether, considering this boy's apparently depressive tone, it might be better to leave it alone.

But, what the hell, he wasn't a Samaritan . . . he was a crotchety old man trying to get on with his things in peace.

"Funny," Puffin said, "I thought I understood your friends barking out something about this being Sparta."

The boy looked perplexed as he glanced back up at Puffin. He pressed his lips tight together and screwed up his eyes as if anticipating a back-handed slap from Puffin . . . and Puffin was of half a mind to give him one.

"You are not gladiators," Puffin said. "It wouldn't make any sense."

The boy held eye contact for a long while before his shoulders arched back, and he gave a hefty, long-winded sigh, blowing out his cheeks as he did so. "Fine," the boy said. "I'll take your word for it then."

Puffin caught a slight chill around the collar of his dressing gown. That feeling he often got when he felt like someone was watching. Usually, though, he got it at home, when he hadn't noticed a cat watching him out of some nook or crevice.

But when he turned around and gazed back up the street, he saw no one there.

Not even a cat.

Puffin looked the boy over, saw how thoroughly fed up he looked, and, if Puffin had somehow been dragged—kicking and screaming—into that same situation, he supposed he might've looked just as dejected.

So maybe that was why Puffin said, "Come on, let's get those ropes off your wrists. I'll boil you up a cup of tea inside, and make up the spare bed."

3

THE RAGGEDY blue rope wasn't difficult to unknot, or Puffin at least made short work of it. He guessed that, given a little time, maybe till dawn, the boy might've wriggled himself free from the streetlight, and waddled off—half-drunk —back home.

Once he'd got the boy free, Puffin had half-expected him to go waddle off up the road, mumbling something incoherent, and thanking Puffin for his offer, but saying no thanks to it finally. But, against Puffin's expectations, the boy kind of drifted along after him.

Up the gravel path. Not so much as wincing as the rocks burrowed into the soles of his bare feet. His lips were a shade of blue, and his eyelids droopy.

Puffin wondered if he'd taken something else during the night's festivities . . . and decided that he—really—couldn't care less.

If there was one thing he knew about the *yoof* it was that they could get over just about any affliction. Except bullets. Bullets *usually* did for them as they did for everyone else.

Still, it was Puffin's belief that the boy just needed rest.

Rest and tea, and he'd be all right again.

Yes, tea was the all-powerful, all-purpose cure. Kind of like sleep, in a way. It was familiar-smelling, and familiar-tasting, and, above all else, warm and soothing.

Not bad for some hot water and some leaves.

As Puffin sat the boy down on one of the fine pine kitchen chairs, and asked him if he took sugar with his tea, the boy gave a solemn nod.

And promptly burst into tears.

Puffin cast a weary glance over him, and then, as he went over to stick the kettle onto the gas stove—he never quite trusted mixing electricity and water . . . at least not at such close quarters —he muttered something to himself about being sorry for having asked.

He let the boy sob his eyes dry, head bowed into his folded arms on the table. And those constant snorts.

Sniff-sniff.

SNORT!

Sniff-sniff

SNORT!

Sniff-sniff . . .

"All right!" Puffin said, "That's enough blubbering for someone your age, didn't you father ever teach you about being a man?" Puffin screwed up his eyes at the boy. "How old *are* you anyway?"

Sniff-sniff.

. . . no *SNORT!* this time, thankfully, and then, "Twenty-free."

"Twenty-three?"

The boy nodded dolefully.

Puffin whistled tunelessly then drummed his fingers on the marble-topped kitchen counter. "My, oh my, to be twenty-*three* again." He shook his head. "My goodness, and what're you sobbing about then?"

The boy swallowed hard, and then looked up. His eyes were glazed with tears. And they shone off his cheeks in the sallow kitchen light. He looked about to say something, but then didn't.

"Come on then," Puffin said. "Out with it or I'll ask you if you want sugar in your tea again."

Sniff-sniff.

SNORT!

"I . . . I, uh," the boy started, his voice wavering whenever he tried to utter anything halfway articulate.

"Out with it, *boy!*"

The boy steadied himself, shoved the bed sheet back up his shoulder, where it had slipped down, and then took a deep breath.

Seemed to gather up a little more confidence in himself. "I tried to kill myself."

"What?"

"Kill myself?"

Puffin thought this over. Thought about just what the boy was telling him, and how it might relate to his current—toga-clad—state. "And why ever did you want to do that?"

The boy shrugged. "Dunno."

The kettle began to bubble, and a coil of steam whistled out from the spout. Without turning his back to the boy, Puffin slipped a pair of porcelain mugs off their gilded, curled wall hooks, and dropped a tea bag in each from the flowery-patterned tin at his elbow.

"That's not a particularly solid reason, now, is it?"

The boy made himself busy with his hands, interlocking and unlocking his fingers from one another. As he did so he pressed his lips tightly together, making odd, contorted faces. "No," he said, "Suppose no'."

Puffin poured the boiling water out from the kettle, listening to that delightful *splash* as it struck the sides of each mug, and then brought the tea bag up, floating, to the surface.

He savoured that first waft of flavour rising up in the air. That warmed-up, little-pouch-of-tea scent. Already he could feel his mouth water with anticipation, and he thought about the doctor who had checked him over, back at that shopping centre, and how he would be extremely pleased that Puffin was slurping on tea rather than endless cups of cocoa.

Perhaps this was the start of a health drive.

But most likely not.

Puffin brought the boy's cup over to the table, set it down on one of the coasters which together, all lined up in a row, formed a panoramic landscape of some coastline or other in Wales.

It looked like whoever had put the pictures together on the

coasters had partaken of some form of computer whizzery seeing as the sky was somehow bleached blue . . . and whenever, back in his youth, he had set off camping in Wales, the sky had invariably been grey, and cloudy, and, above all else, *wet*.

Still, they were decent, serviceable coasters.

And it seemed easy enough to believe that they would outlive him.

Just like his will.

Puffin wrapped his hands about the warm cup, and stared over its rim at the boy, who was concentrating now on his own mug, and the mulchy-coloured contents.

The boy at least seemed a better colour now. His cheeks weren't quite so puffy. And his eyes seemed a little sharper than they had seemed while he'd been out there all tied up to that lamppost.

"Go on, then," Puffin said.

The boy stared down into the mug, and the steam rose up in the kitchen air. He sighed again, and Puffin started to wonder whether all this sighing might be the thing that was causing him all the trouble . . . or *apparent* trouble . . . in his life.

"The boys," he started, "they were jus' trying to cheer me up, you know. They found out, or, well, they didn' find out abou' me trying to kill myself, but they knew I was done, know wha' I mean?"

Puffin arched an eyebrow. "I can't say that I do."

The boy sighed hard again. "Been a load a hard trucking, you know, last few weeks, and tha'."

"And why would that be?"

"Everything's just been shit, tha's wha'."

Puffin sipped at his still-too-hot tea. He felt it scold his lips, and then his tongue, and then his throat, and then . . . well, wherever it went next . . . right on down to the pit of his stomach. After a couple of gulps, Puffin said, "*Do* elaborate."

The boy shook his head and gave Puffin a wry smile across the table. "Nah," he said, "nah, don' reckon you'd understand it, no' at all."

"Try me."

Still shaking his head, the boy took a sip of his own tea. And Puffin watched on as the boy experienced just what Puffin had: scolded lips, burned tongue, fried throat, scarred insides. Then, just like Puffin, he recovered.

"Jus' ain' been doing well, if you know wha' I mean? Firs' I get kicked off my job, and that, and nex' thing I know I jus' can' find anything at all, nuffink worth doing, anyway."

Puffin squinted at the boy as if that might make it easier to decipher his *thick* accent. The way that kids spoke these days was really on the cusp of getting beyond him. And Puffin thought that he'd spent a good proportion of his life . . . which was to say, a much *larger* proportion of his life than he would've wanted . . . with kids, *trying* to instil some sense of academic wonder into them . . . and mostly failing.

"Well," Puffin said, "what qualifications do you have?"

"Qualifications?"

"Yes, you know, ABCs, the numbers one to a hundred—adding and subtracting, if you can *really* grasp it. Multiplication and division too if you've got your heart set on a Nobel Prize."

"Noble wha'?"

"Never mind," Puffin said, feeling himself getting caught up in the flow of conversation . . . or being overwhelmed by the desire to hear his own voice, which happened nearly as often. "The thing is that you've got to realise your situation *probably* isn't quite as hopeless as you imagine."

The boy puffed out his cheeks. Sighed hard . . . *again*. "Got that right, don' even know how to kill myself proper."

"Proper*ly*."

"Yeah," the boy said, with a wry smile, "jus' wha' my teachers said, and all, innit?"

"Just out of interest, how *did* you try to kill yourself?"

"Pills, innit?"

"And what went wrong?"

Another wry smile, then, "Learned you can't overdose yourself on Vitamin C."

4

AFTER the first cup of tea, Puffin noticed the slight stirrings in both his, and his guest's, belly. And so he decided, it being nigh on five in the morning, and the dawn already sparking up, turning the night sky a shade of pink, that a spot of breakfast was in order.

He studied the boy, caught him yawning a few times, and then shaking his head vigorously, as if to try and keep himself awake.

Puffin located several packets of bacon from within the deeper recesses of his fridge, and he peeled them out, slice by slice. And then he plucked out a few eggs, a packet of sausages. A tin of beans. And he felt his stomach quibble with anticipation.

One of the cats poked its head around the corner to the kitchen, nose twitching. But, with one glance to the boy sitting at the kitchen table, it retreated back . . . shifted back off to the chair, apparently waiting for Puffin to return, and for the stranger to go.

As Puffin sat back down at the kitchen table, with the crackling of the bacon and sausages in the grill, and the frying of the egg on the stove, and all those wonderful, meaty, and buttery smells wafting about the dawning kitchen, he waited for the boy to continue.

When he didn't Puffin thought it his role to prompt him. "And what is it that your 'boys' all do then? I mean, to *earn* a living?"

The boy shrugged. "Mechanics, and tha'."

"Well, that's a decent living, you can make a decent living doing that. You should see my last service receipt for my car. They can't be doing too badly. Why don't you ask one of them to put a word in for you?"

"Don' like cars."

"Is that so?"

"Uh huh."

"Well, what do the others do?"

"Gardeners, shop assistants, got a mate that sells batteries to people."

"And none of them have got any contacts they can help you with?"

"You wha'?"

"*Contacts*," Puffin said, with greater emphasis this time. "You know, people who can help you get your foot on the rung, give you a start in a trade, *that* sort of thing?"

"Nah," the boy said.

"And why not?"

"Dunno," the boy said, and Puffin was on the point of prompting him, of *pushing* him to explore just why he believed that before he carried on himself, "I ain' good with my hands or nuffink. Don' know numbers, shi' at spellings and stuff. Ain' nuffink much I can do, you get me?"

"Yes, well, I think I do 'get you', fairly well."

"Yeah," the boy said, wiggling his nose just a little, and glancing off in the direction of their cooking breakfasts.

Puffin served up their bacon and sausages, and eggs, and did some toast too. And he made another cup of tea, and once he was done with it, they both sat down and ate in silence.

Silence except for the *scrape* of cutlery on porcelain, and the munching chews, the sucking swallows as they took their breakfasts down.

And Puffin felt his stomach grumbling with content as it digested, and could still taste those sweet tastes in his mouth, and all those fats oozing about his mouth, making him feel as snug as a blue whale must feel after it's gobbled up a lion's share of krill.

"Anyway," the boy said, laying his cutlery down on his plate with a huge *clatter*, "wha' d'you do tha's so special, eh? Why've you got this fancy house?"

On another day, another morning, Puffin might well have

given the boy a clip round the ear. He realised why he'd never had children in the first place. All they did was talk back, probe away with impertinent questions.

"I was a teacher," Puffin said.

The boy screwed up his eyes. "Yeah, but a teacher don' earn all tha' much."

Puffin felt his gut twist a little. His stomach perhaps protesting all at once at the sudden influx of food. But he kept his face straight . . . as straight as he could keep it without blowing up in this kid's face.

Just who did he think he was?

If it hadn't been for Puffin, no doubt this dullard would still be sitting out there in his bed sheet, snoring away with his hands tied round the back of the lamppost.

But Puffin kept a handle on his temper, which he'd found easier and easier with each passing year he'd spent *outside* the classroom.

The thing was that, after forty years' teaching kids, he'd realised that he was something like allergic to them.

"Well?" the boy said, squinting a little, elbows resting on the table, a splatter of baked bean sauce glistening off his lips from the fledgling sunrays beaming into the kitchen.

"My wife," Puffin started, "she was, well, she was a very successful lawyer."

"Lawyer?"

"Yes, well, it's a person who—"

"Dontcha be smar' with me. I know wha' a lawyer is. Fine, I migh' no' be able to spell good, or wha'ever, but I seen some TV, I've had some friends wha've been in cour' and tha', and you's telling me she was one of them?"

Puffin noted all the creases that had formed about the boy's eyes, and he realised that telling him just what his wife had been might not have been the best decision he'd made that evening . . . that *morning*.

"Yeah," the boy continued, "I know all abou' lawyers, and tha'."

Puffin strained a smile, and then went to pick up their plates. Though the boy had more or less *licked* his own plate clean of all its sauce, Puffin's still had a few pieces of bacon fat, scraps of sausage, and toast crusts left over.

He deposited the remains of his breakfast into the bin, getting that waft of rubbish juice as he propped back the chrome lid. His tongue felt truly contented now, nice and lolled up in his mouth, warm and flaccid. And his whole body seemed to glow, hardly noticing the bite of the morning chill.

With a *thud*, he flipped the bin shut, and dropped the plates in the sink for washing up later on. As he sat back down at the table, the boy seated opposite him with his half-finished mug of tea still clasped in his hands, Puffin thought about just what he was going to say next, and before he'd so much as given it a run-through in his mind, he found himself saying it right out loud.

"Look here, I never got your name, what is it?"

"Hugh."

"Hugh," Puffin said, trying it out, and then, "well, listen here, Hugh, what about if I propose something for you . . . some arrangement?"

"Yeah?" the boy said, dark bags drooping down from his eyes, but his eyebrows rising out of interest.

"How would you like me to teach you some of those things, you know, *things* that might help you with exams, for qualifications?"

The boy remained open-mouthed for a few moments. And then, slowly but surely, his mouth creased right out into a smile. "Tha'd be, I dunno, pritty mental, mate."

Puffin wondered exactly what the boy . . . what *Hugh*, meant when he said, 'mental', but he supposed that it meant 'good', or as near to as to make the exact meaning insignificant.

"Great," Puffin said, giving him a light smile of his own, and still unable to comprehend just what he'd said . . . and *why* he'd said it.

Why, he'd spent the whole time, ever since his wife had died, just trying to get shot of other *people*. But now, just acting on instinct, he'd extended this offer.

Hugh knitted his brows together and stared down into his mug of tea. "One thing, though, righ'?"

"And what's that?" Puffin said.

"Can' pay you, man."

Puffin thought this over. When he'd extended the offer, he'd never dreamed of asking for payment, though now he realised that, by the nature of the arrangement, it'd be pretty strange for him not to ask for *something* in return.

But, really, he had no use for money.

All it did was sit in a bank account and soak up interest.

But maybe he *could* find something for Hugh to do . . . yes, something basic, something that he would understand. And, finally, he arrived at the very thing.

"How about you do some garden work for me? You see, with my back, with my old, frail body, I don't get about as much as I used to . . . especially with the *heavy* lifting, I could use some real help."

Hugh jabbed his tongue into his cheek, making it bulge outwards. "Dunno much 'bout gardens."

"Oh, really, there's nothing to them at all. Believe me. It's second nature. And it'd be a good opportunity for you to—you know—pick up another *skill* to try something new. You can't be put off learning new things, you know?"

Hugh still remained a little unconvinced, his lips pursed, and eyes wandering about the kitchen.

Puffin thought back to his kids when he'd been at school, and .. . though it brought him out in cold sweats . . . he thought specifically back to the bad kids, the late kids, the kids who swore and fought, and spat, and . . . well, got up to all sorts really.

And the one thing that had united them, had united *all* of them, had been their fear of learning.

He remembered that now. It was like their parents had beat them around the head with their own school textbooks from the moment they were born.

That was Hugh's problem . . . and it'd only taken this little encounter for Puffin to remember it.

But he remembered it *now*.

"It'll be fine," Puffin said, hearing his own voice sounding far more sympathetic, far *softer*, than he had ever heard it before. "I promise it'll be fine."

And Hugh raised his head, his wide eyes to Puffin's, and that same old, dependable smile returned to his face. And Puffin, once more, knew that there was something to live for.

Something to give back to the world.

5

PUFFIN PACED his front hall at four o'clock on Thursday afternoon. The grandfather clock in the hall ticked along, its pendulum making a dull chime as it reached the top of its arc.

The sunny afternoon light wafted in through the frosted-glass of the window, and warmed Puffin's skin. Warmed his *blood*.

The air was thick with the smell of furniture polish since Puffin had spent most of the day cleaning house, for some reason feeling like he wanted to make a good impression on Hugh when he came round for his lessons.

Though, right now, as he paced, he couldn't think *why* that was.

The furniture polish was so thick that Puffin could almost taste its tang on his tongue, in there with the constant feel of fur against his skin from the constantly shedding cats about the house.

Either because they expected a visitor, or because of the grand cleaning ritual, the cats had all made themselves scarce. He'd happened on them all in the airing cupboard . . . having snuck inside through the door that never shut completely.

That was their favourite hiding place.

Puffin glanced at the clock.

Quarter past four.

They'd agreed that Hugh would be over here by four o'clock, and so it was certainly an extremely poor start for him to be arriving late, to his *first* lesson.

But then a worse eventuality struck Puffin. And it was so wretched that he almost beat it right out of his mind, like a wisp of unwanted dust, before it had the chance to fully germinate.

What if Hugh wouldn't come?

What if that meeting had all been some odd—*extremely* odd— waking dream?

Though Puffin had always considered himself a more or less

lucid fellow, there was no telling whether or not he might've taken a wrong turn down the spiral stairs into Crazyville.

Goodness knew, it'd happened to the rest of his family.

His brother, his sister, his mother, his father.

Could that be it?

But even then Puffin realised that his going crazy paled in comparison to his scheduled meeting today with Hugh. He had built up his entire week towards it.

Waited it out for the longest time.

And it would seem so . . . so . . . *cruel* for it to be wrenched from his grasp at the last.

But wasn't this what he'd asked for?

What he'd *always* wanted?

Now he had his peace and quiet, his cats, he could walk about all day in his dressing gown doing whatever the hell he *damn well* pleased.

Had that really been living, though? Or just waiting to die?

He looked at himself in the, now well-polished, full-length hall mirror.

He had decided today to put on a pair of smart, navy-blue corduroy trousers, and to wear a pristine white shirt—the same shirt he had worn to his wife's funeral, and never since.

His shoes, too, were shined-up to a full walnut brown.

All that considering that some days, while he mooched about the house, it would've been a wonder, a *really* special day, if he was to have so much as a shower.

Yes, it was all clear to him now, staring him in the face. He truly *had* built this up to be something special.

And now, at the last moment, it was to be taken from him.

The clock now read twenty-five past four, and it seemed to be ticking on harder, its pendulum beating him on, like a whip between the shoulder blades, dragging him closer to death.

And he didn't *want* to die.

As he thought about returning upstairs, to take off his trousers, and his white shirt, and hanging everything back up in its respective thick, plastic laundry bag, he heard the familiar metal *clatter* of his front garden gate swinging open.

His heart bobbed up in his throat. And he felt his blood pump harder. Faster. Almost overwhelming his conscious thoughts with . . . with—*yes*—it wasn't too strong of a term, was it?

Happiness.

And as the sound of footsteps reached a fever pitch and then promptly stopped on the front doorstep, and the outline of Hugh shone through the frosted glass, his silhouette backed by the gleaming afternoon sunlight, Puffin couldn't help but press a wide smile onto his lips.

He opened the door with a *creak* of the hinges and felt the warmth of the sun against his skin.

And it felt wonderful.

NOBODY LIKES A QUITTER

1

BEN'S spit tasted of nothing.

Was that what frost tasted like?

The sour stench of sweat, mixed with the chilly air, singed his nostrils.

All that broke the silence was the gentle *rustle* of sports clothing against skin.

Scattered all about them were bright, white, brand-new footballs.

Round and plastic-looking and gleaming with dew.

Oh how Ben longed to give one of them a good kick, into one of the empty goals, to hear it nestle in there, against the net.

But there was little prospect of that.

Not while they were in fitness training.

Gearing up for the long—*hard*—matches to come.

The late-November turf was frozen stiff. And the blades of grass were like shards of broken glass prodding between Ben's fingers. As he brought himself down another inch, down so that his chin made contact with the iced-over earth, he heard the coach's voice thick and hard once more.

"Come on, boys! Nobody likes a quitter!"

Ben pushed himself up even further still, feeling the tug on his muscles from the push-up. At the top of his push-up, he felt like he couldn't go any further, that he had reached the Limit.

The Limit was something that they all talked about, all of them on the football team.

It was that time when you couldn't possibly put one foot in front of the other without either tipping over and collapsing like a freshly cut birch tree, or puking all over the place.

And Ben felt somewhere caught in between those two sensations.

And neither of those would go down well with the boys.

Ben held himself up, his arms aching so hard now.

Fifty-three.

Fifty-three push-ups.

Was that so bad?

Oh, sure, the coach had chewed into them this whole thing about the hundred-push-up challenge, that every single member of the team was to get through to the end of it.

Every member of the team was *expected* to hit exactly *one hundred* push-ups.

But, for what?

What was the point of it?

What would it achieve?

Was there some sort of god above them, some galactic emperor that . . .

"Hodds!" the coach shouted out.

His voice sent a shimmer along Ben's spine, but he could do nothing to stop the way that he felt. In short, he was done. He had gone and reached the Limit and that was that.

Still, Ben continued to stare down at the turf before him. His hands had long ago gone all numb, and he tried his best, while still supporting his weight on his palms, to give his fingertips a wiggle. Though he watched them move, he couldn't feel them at all.

He could sense the coach standing over him.

He could picture him in his mind.

Baseball cap pulled *way* down over his eyes. Those tufts of grey hair protruding out the sides. That three-day stubble all gathered about his cheeks.

He probably had his hands on his hips.

And he was no doubt masticating something.

Chewing gum?

Who knew?

All that Ben knew was that the coach was *always* chewing . . .

what it might be inside that hot-breathed, halitosis-stinking mouth of his, he couldn't say.

"Hodds?" the coach said, this time his voice at a lower tone, but, somehow, more insistent.

Ben took in a deep breath, composed himself. He felt his shoulders rise and then fall, and then he allowed his arms to let go. He felt the turf brush his chin another time.

Then he heaved himself up once more.

Fifty-four.

As Ben channelled himself into the rest of the team around him, each of them vocalising their own current repetition, he heard a whole bunch of *seventies* . . . and even a couple of *eighties* . . .

"You wanna spend the rest of the season in the reserves, Hodds?"

Ben held himself at his fifty-fourth push-up.

He stared down at the frozen ground.

His mind swirled a little.

He thought back to his cereal that morning.

It had been honey-flavoured, with little slices of peaches all perched on the top.

Since he was a night owl, he had to trick himself into waking up early, to coming to these early-morning training sessions. He had to give himself something to look forwards to, and that honey-flavoured cereal, that whole-tasting coffee, and those twin slices of toast—all smothered with peanut butter—those things were his motivation.

Just thinking about it now, he was almost sure that he could smell somebody throwing together seconds. Perhaps they were. Over his shoulder. Back at the clubhouse. Back where they'd all got themselves changed just half an hour ago.

"Hodds?" the coach said, yet again making his tone sound more insistent and *yet* even more muffled.

Ben stared down at the pale-blue tinge that was creeping over the surface of his skin, and it was in that moment that the shudder passed through his blood. When it ran all the way around his veins and then centred on his heart.

It gave him a jolt.

And Ben collapsed forwards, on his front, panting to himself.

Straightaway, without giving Ben a moment for a break, the coach was right down on him, in his ear, "You get yourself up *right now* and you go do twenty laps of the pitch."

Ben continued to lie there, on his front, as he listened to the *crunch* of the coach walking away from him, back across the frozen turf. The chill which had descended over Ben now seemed so complete as to wrap him up into a little ball of cotton.

Was this what his life had come to?

Was this what chasing his dream had come to?

. . . Chasing a hundred press-ups that he couldn't possibly do, and then, to top it all off, having to do twenty laps of the football pitch?

It was then that it hit Ben.

When he knew what he must do.

Suddenly, as soon as the idea sank in with him, Ben felt a warmth spreading through his blood, making its way to the surface of his skin, and he pictured that sensation working to melt away the layer of frost which lay on the surface of the grass.

Slowly, he helped himself onto his knees.

And then he stood.

He looked out over the penitent bodies, going about their one-hundred press-up challenge, and then he sought out the coach, watched him striding in his short shorts, jaw constantly chewing, clipboard pinned beneath his arm.

Ben drew in a deep breath, and then let it out.

"Coach?" Ben said.

The coach paused at one of Ben's teammates, took a quick

glance at the teammate, listening to his progress on his press-up repetitions, and then he cocked his head in Ben's direction.

"If you don't get your arse hopping about that pitch then I'll have you training with the under-sevens, that clear?"

Ben felt his chest tighten. But he knew himself.

Better than *coach* knew him anyway.

"I quit, coach," Ben said, and then he traipsed off in the direction of the dressing rooms, already with that thought of a second breakfast materialising in his mind's eye.

2

BACK HOME, in bed, all tucked up with blankets either side of him, and a box of his favourite cereal open in his lap, Ben surfed the channels, trying to find something to entertain himself. He crunched on his cereal, savouring those honey notes of it. He breathed in that thick stench of his own room, of the deodorant, and that slightly damp smell of sweat, on account of his sports kit which he'd dumped over in the corner.

He skipped the channels, from the news, to the sitcoms, to the chat shows, but he couldn't find anything in particular that he could focus on.

Feeling a slight draught blowing on in beneath his bedroom door, Ben drew his blankets up tighter about himself. He dug his hand into his box of cereal and brought out another handful which he quickly shoved into his mouth.

As he crunched away on it, he heard his mobile buzzing its way across his bedside table. He glanced casually at the screen. Saw that it was Billy . . . one of his teammates.

He muted the TV with the remote and then picked up the call.

"Hello?" Ben said, making his focus go all blurry so that the pictures of the TV were just reduced to a whole bunch of muddy colours.

"Ben?" Billy said, on the other end.

"Yeah?"

"Did you really quit?" Billy said. "I mean, it was *serious* . . . not a joke, or anything?"

"Nope," Ben said, with a slight smile, still staring at the TV screen.

A long silence yawned open between the two of them, and Ben was certain that he could hear the microprocessor of his mobile buzzing away . . . or maybe it was some static on the phone line between himself and Billy.

"I . . . I don't understand," Billy said. "Was it about the challenge? Because you couldn't do the press-up challenge? Was that the reason?"

Ben shrugged even though he knew that Billy couldn't see him. "Yeah, sort of."

He pictured Billy, in his mind's eye, with lips slightly parted, looking thoroughly confused.

"Do you, uh," Billy said, "want to go get a drink later on, talk a bit more about it?"

Ben brought the TV back into focus, but, finding the picture too sharp for his liking, the colours *far too bright*, he shut his eyes.

He had taken the decision. He had wanted to divorce himself from everything that had come before . . . but—*dammit*—he had known, even then, that it would be impossible.

He *had* to explain himself to others.

To others . . .

And so he agreed to Billy's request for a 'drink later on', and then hung up.

As Ben slouched about, in bed, allowing the pictures from the TV to ebb into his mind and rumble around in there, he couldn't help but allow himself a dirty great big grin.

3

A T FOUR O'CLOCK that Sunday afternoon, the pub was absolutely rammed.

A stale stench of spilled ale stuck to the place.

Almost right away Ben tasted a sour note in his mouth.

Though it had taken him a long time to realise it—and maybe now was the first time that he was *really* acknowledging it consciously—he now noted that he *hated* alcohol.

He hated everything about it. About how it made his head sore. About how it made him *dehydrated*. About how it made him do stupid shit.

Shit that he always—*without exception*—greatly regretted the morning after.

But he was here now, and there wasn't anything to do about it.

So he elbowed his way through the *babble* of the crowd and over to the table in the corner where, he saw, Billy was already waiting for him.

All ginger-haired, and wearing a dark-purple shirt, open down to his well-defined, and well-shaved, pectoral muscles.

Billy hadn't yet seen him, and he was staring off to his side, apparently fixated a middle-aged man at the bar's loose backside, held firmly in place by a pair of jeans at least a couple of sizes too small.

As Ben approached, Billy continued to appear engrossed, before he curled his hand about his pint and brought it up to his lips. He sucked at his pint pensively and then, as if he had sensed Ben's presence through telepathy, he glanced up.

Smiled.

Albeit just a little apprehensively.

As Ben took his place on the flimsy little knee-high stool across the table from Billy, he knew just what Billy was thinking. That he was worried about him . . . as his *friend* . . . that he was having a funny turn, or whatever. He speculated as to the depth of Billy's thoughts, if he, maybe, thought that this was the sort of way somebody might act before they were about to have an aneurysm, or if they were about to do something *totally crazy* . . . like quit the football team that had been the crux of their life for as long as could be remembered.

Ben did have to admit that, from the outside, his decision *did* look just a tad crazy.

Not that he had any doubts about what he'd done.

They chatted for a little while about what had happened when Ben had left, how everybody had reacted. How one of their teammates had said that he'd seen Ben grinning to himself . . . another had seen him punching a locker on his way to the dressing room.

Ben knew neither of these observations to be correct.

He could quite plainly remember that he had kept himself thoroughly stoic—just totally *unfeeling* and *expressionless*—all the way to his peg in the dressing room.

Why, he hadn't actually smiled till he'd got back to his bedroom, got himself all tucked up, not till he'd hung the phone up on Billy, to tell the truth.

"So," Billy said, with only the dregs of his pint remaining, which he swilled about in the bottom of the glass and stared into like a psychic about to tell a fortune with tea leaves, "why'd you quit the team?"

Ben looked over Billy's head, to the slot machine there. To its bright yellow lights that shone differently depending on the coloured paper which sat over each button. He watched the wheels toying with themselves, spinning around as they attempted to lure potential gamers from the crowd.

Just one pound, they seemed to say. *Just one pound is all it takes.*

Ben brought Billy back into focus, noted the firm expression of concern sketched all over his best friend's face. Ben gave a shrug, brought his pint up to his lips, and knocked back what remained there. He set the glass down on the dark-red, lacquered surface of the table, in a previously staked-out beer ring, and said, "Do you remember, back when we were kids?"

Billy squinted at him, as if a heavy fog had set in between them. "Remember what?" he said.

Ben pressed his lips together, tasted again the sour ale, and felt his mouth watering for more, though his brain told him that he required water. It was stupid—a body—almost like a device which had a built-in conflict. Something intrinsic about itself which would never allow it to find *true* freedom.

"You remember," Ben said, allowing those words to linger a little, in the air between them, "You remember about how we talked about going travelling?"

Now apparently on firmer ground, Billy gave a slight smile, though he turned back to stare into his empty pint glass, as if he might be able to magically replenish its contents. "Yeah?"

"Well, do you remember when I talked to you about going to . . ." Ben paused for a second, his eyes flickered about him—*why*, he wasn't entirely sure, apart from this deep feeling within himself that somebody might be eavesdropping on them, ". . . *Tibet*," he added finally.

"Tibet?" Billy said, his eyes widening. "What d'you want to go to *Tibet* for?"

Ben held himself very still.

He had expected this reaction—could've predicted it *easily*.

But that didn't make things any easier.

Didn't mean that he could plan what to say next with any exactitude.

"What the fuck's in Tibet?" Billy said, this time with a tone of anger to his voice.

Ben allowed himself a half smile. He shifted a gaze off into the crowd of people about the bar, to all of those middle-aged men who clutched their pints of reddish ale, who were all *red* in the face, and who all seemed to have that *redness* about their eyes as if they were perpetually *too tired* to do anything.

Families?

Wives?

Kids?

Was that what it was all about?

. . . If it was, then Ben would have nothing more to do with it.

Without another word to Billy, Ben hoisted himself up off his stool, rolled his shoulders, still attempting to rid himself of those muscular aches that'd been brought on by the press-ups that morning. Before he left the table, he thanked Billy for the drink, and then asked him if he wanted to see him off at the airport the following day.

Billy said nothing.

Didn't even look back at him.

Just shook his head slightly mumbling, beneath his breath, "Fucking Tibet, what the fuck's in Tibet?"

4

B EN PACKED UP all his gear for his new life.

There wasn't much to get in, all told.

For the new life that he had got lined up for himself, he wouldn't need *anything* . . . but, still, he couldn't help but retain an attachment to some of his worldly goods.

A yellowed, faded photograph of himself and his dad, with his hands on a Player of the Season trophy, the first one that Ben had won. The trophy itself had long ago been thrown out. He also took along a necklace of his mother's, the only thing that he had retained of hers, much to his siblings' disbelief.

They had been after the house.

The savings.

And the pair of—hardly used—cars parked up in the drive.

But Ben hadn't needed any of that stuff.

It would only weigh him down.

He had known that, even back then.

And he knew it, more than ever, *now*.

His mother's necklace was a gilded locket and, within, there was a tiny scrap of a pearl which sat opposite a picture of Ben and his mother.

He wondered if his mother had ever told his siblings—ever let them *know*—whose picture was actually nestled behind the thin glass of her locket.

His gut feeling that she had not . . . perhaps she hadn't even told Ben's father.

Ben couldn't fathom why she would have told anybody else.

Because his connection with his mother was beyond *their* comprehension.

With the locket squeezed in one hand, and the photograph with his father in the other, Ben hoisted his rucksack up onto his shoulder.

The rucksack—of course—was stuffed full of clothes. He couldn't get by without them. Not for the first few days, anyway, the days that it would take him to get himself on up to Tibet . . . to get himself onto the high road and aimed, squarely, for his new life.

But, that aside, he left his bedroom very much as it was.

His housemates would dig through his things when they realised that he was gone, that he wasn't coming back, and, if *they* didn't, then he knew—eventually—his landlord would.

With his goodbyes to his bedroom done, he trudged on out of the house, and caught a bus to the airport.

5

A S BEN absorbed the bright—*too bright*—fluorescent lights of the terminal, breathed in the sharp scent of bleach which seemed to cling to the place so relentlessly, he glanced about himself, looked about the crowds, seeing if he couldn't pick up a tuft of red hair someplace.

Some sign that Billy had come to see him off.

But he couldn't.

Ben couldn't say that he was surprised.

He couldn't say that he was depressed about the fact either . . . because, perhaps, all that this showed was that Billy had realised, when they'd been speaking in the pub, just how thoroughly Ben had divorced himself from his former life.

He had a new path ahead of him.

Just opening up.

Lighting his way forwards.

And he would be nothing but a fool to ignore it.

Ben listened to the strange electronic jingles which preceded each announcement on the PA system, those sounds that were designed to attract attention to the message which followed. But when the messages did follow, they were muffled—*garbled almost*—at least to Ben's ears, and he wondered if they were intended for anybody to hear at all.

Or if they were mere Scotch mist.

As he joined the snaking queue which led to Passport Control, Ben heard somebody calling out his name. He didn't need to turn to know just who it was. Just who had come to meet him here, at the airport, right now.

He did turn to look, though.

And, sure enough, he saw Billy there.

His red hair almost aflame in this otherwise bland and white-

124

washed space.

For a long few moments, they said nothing at all.

And Ben wondered if Billy regretted having come here.

He wished to tell him that he didn't *need* to be here, that he wasn't a *necessary* part of the process, but something in his gut told him to hold back, that he wouldn't be able to phrase just what he had to say so easily.

Not in words.

As Ben took in Billy properly this time, as Billy hugged him, he noticed that he wore a rucksack too. When Ben withdrew from Billy he saw that he had a passport clutched in his fist.

Billy grinned from ear to ear as he saw Ben noticing.

"What's this?" Ben said.

Billy continued to grin, apparently unshakable now.

Whatever it was that he had got his mind snagged on, he simply wouldn't let it go.

"I'm coming along too," Billy said.

Ben felt his chest tighten. His gut dipped just a tiny bit. He looked about him, as if he might see his teammates all standing by, ready to pile on in at this joke . . . or whatever it was that was going on right now.

But there was nobody about who Ben recognised.

And certainly no members of his team.

He brought Billy back into focus, feeling his brow wrinkling up in confusion. "Why d'you want to come to Tibet?" Ben said.

Billy continued to grin away, and gave a shrug. "Dunno, something to do, I guess, we've got the holidays ahead of us—why not?"

Ben glanced about again, still not quite sure he could believe what his best friend was telling him—that he, *really*, intended to come along with him.

"You've got a ticket?" Ben said.

Billy nodded.

"For the same flight?"

"Same one you said you'd be flying out on."

Ben held still, not sure what to say, whether he should be flattered, or whether he should be horrified. He had spent so much of the last few hours saying goodbye to his old life, stubbornly putting one foot in front of the other as he headed into the new.

But some parts wanted to hold on.

Billy wanted to hold on.

Billy appeared to detect this indecision, and he frowned. "Everything all right?"

Ben knew that he couldn't lie to his best friend. That he couldn't simply *take him along* without him knowing the truth. And so, eyeing the coffee shop which stood off to one side of them, he put his arm about his friend and took him off there, to go and tell him how things were.

It took about ten minutes to make his meaning clear, to make his meaning as clear as he could make it to Billy.

And Ben expected—over all else—and just from judging the ever-changing look of confusion smeared all across Billy's face, that Billy would see reason.

But, right at the last, when the announcement for Ben's flight crackled over the PA, Billy continued to tag along with him.

Ben couldn't quite believe it.

In fact he was struck dumb.

"What're you doing?" Ben said.

Billy raised a faint smile to him and answered, "Coming along."

Ben eyed the queue to Passport Control, readied himself for departure from here, from his home, from everything he'd ever known. And yet with his best friend at his side.

Ben found himself smiling back at Billy, his heart rapping a little in his chest as he said, "Are you quite sure? Nobody likes a quitter, after all."

WHEN THE PRIME MINISTER SNEEZES

W HEN THE PRIME MINISTER sneezes I'm the one that comes running, looking all prim and tidy in my navy-blue suit jacket, with a crisp-white, freshly-laundered handkerchief out and ready to pass into his hand. And he always takes it from me with that same plump-cheeked, ripe smile of his, and that mumbled, "Thanks," before he turns back to whatever crowd or whatever foreign dignitary he's addressing at that moment in time.

And when I catch sight of beads of sweat forming on his forehead I'm ready with another handkerchief, a fresh one, always, that he takes from me and uses to dab the sweat away. Sometimes, when I get back home, to my studio flat in evening, I've forgotten to drop the handkerchief off at the prime-ministerial laundry service and so I have to pop it in with the rest of my washing. The whites, of course, the ones that I stick in on a sixty-degree cycle so that it's just as fresh and bouncy as anything that's run through the prime-ministerial service.

Once he came down with a nosebleed, quite out of nowhere, although I do remember it happened just as we were stepping down off a plane, coming down the steps, and I suppose the stress, or the altitude of our destination, got to him, and the blood just started running.

I was there of course, ready to oblige him with a fresh hanky.

That was one of the few handkerchiefs that I've disposed of, the one that had that metallic stench lingering on it, the one that I knew impulsively that no amount of cleaning would take care of. That particular handkerchief just ended up in a bin sitting on the runway, and we left it behind when we took our leave later in the day.

I've caught something of a reputation for being the 'man with the handkerchief' down the years the prime minister's been in office.

I first started out serving the prime minister when I began as a junior assistant, back when he was a mere candidate, and I was serving on his campaign for the prime minister's job. And I remember that first day I met him, the first time I had been in the same room as him.

I recall very clearly how I'd watched his nostrils flare and his mouth gape wide, and before I'd so much as given the matter any thought, I bucked forwards, unfurling a handkerchief my mother had given me that morning to stick in the breast pocket of my suit to give my appearance something of a note of style.

While I wasn't totally convinced as to the style, I suppose that the handkerchief served just fine since I was able to unfurl it at that moment's notice and thrust it before the prime minister as he glared down at the assorted phlegm sticking to his hands.

I recall that spark at the edge of his eye as he glanced and then double glanced at me, and then gave me a wry smile as he accepted the handkerchief, dried his hands with it, and then, with a brief pause, perhaps wondering just whether or not he might be acting in some impertinent manner, he passed the handkerchief back to me.

And it seemed that I no longer had to paddle my legs trying to stay afloat.

Because it seemed that I'd finally found my place among the prime minister's backroom team. And the City, and all its glories, the tidy studio flats and its polished-up chauffeured cars, with tinted windows, were all mine to reflect in.

Today I stand behind the prime minister at the funeral of his wife. This morning, as I passed by the prime-ministerial laundry, I decided to pick out a dozen or so handkerchiefs, since I knew that this would be something of an emotive moment for my employer.

I breathe in the cool stone of the church, and that stilted dust, which seems forever rising in the room of any holy-appointed building, settles in my airways and, inevitably, on the back of my tongue. My heart beats calmly and evenly, but I can still feel its wrenching action pounding the blood about my circulatory system. And I can hear the prime minister's heavy breathing, and that slight nasal *tick* as the phlegm at the back of his throat threatens to spill out into a full-force sneeze.

The prime minister stands before me, his shoulders arched, and his head tilted downwards to his chest, in a posture suggesting long-built up grief. And I prepare myself for whenever the moment is going to come, when the first tear worms its way down his cheek . . . or when that well-held sneeze finally breaks out.

However, I find myself somewhat dismayed . . . no, not dismayed, because how can I be disappointed not to catch a glimpse of my employer crying? . . . No the feeling is more one of surprise.

What could possibly have led him not to grieve openly, not to sob out his lungs for his dearly departed?

Then I consider his position, his position here among the congregation, and I take in the ministers, the *opposition* politicians, and I know that even this, this most *private* of moments, must be spun out, toyed with, and used to plump up his statesman's figure.

Because one moment, one flinching half-second of weakness, would be all it would take to bring the prime minister, and by extension, the country to its knees.

And the last thing the country needs right now is to be brought down to its knees.

We must stick together, all of us, else we *fall* together.

The coffin stands before us, raised above us, and the archbishop stands still at its side, his grey cheeks and hard, sheeny eyes glare to the stone-slabbed floor at his feet. Over our heads the notes of the organ drift about, bathing us in its mournful tones: that tone of the deathly world exacting itself on that of the living.

The last connection.

The last breath.

The archbishop snaps his chin upwards and addresses the congregation, passing his eyes over seemingly everyone assembled there, and yet lingering over precisely no one. When he catches my eye, he looks away before I think to do the same myself.

I wonder whether he has rehearsed the mournful tone of voice he strikes a thousand times while stood before a mirror. Because I know what it means to be practised, how to know your role inside and out, and today, of all days, with not just the media watching—but the *international* media watching—he must strike that most difficult and sturdy of postures.

The bridgeman to the Land of the Living, giving us that glance into the Land of the Dead.

My eyes, of course, hardly drift off the shoulder blades of the prime minister standing before me, and I know that I must stay attuned to every slight tremor, each and every muffled sob, and to any hint that *I* might be required to sidle up to him, handkerchief in hand, ready to give him something of the dignity that our leader requires to retain something of his modesty.

But he just stands still. Apparently unmoved by the spectacle. At least from where I'm standing.

We take our seats, myself on the hard, wooden bench, a few along from the prime minister, but close enough so that I might be able to get a handkerchief to him if he needs it.

If he feels the need to put his emotions on show.

But he simply sits there, chin just upright, and absorbs the words from the archbishop as they ebb out over the heads of the congregation.

And I lose myself in those same words too. Feel them wash over me, like a winter mist on a pebble beach.

And that chill that runs round my collar.

The service reaches its conclusion almost before I've had a chance to fully immerse myself in it. The prime minister stays seated throughout, not wishing to go up to the pulpit and say something, a word—*anything*—about his wife, and I study him from his profile, trying to see a stitch of emotion, something that shows the impact of the service upon him.

But he gives nothing away at all, and before I know it, the archbishop is concluding the service with a prayer, and the organ is playing once more, and everyone is standing.

Some of the congregation is leaving, and all along I keep my gaze fixed onto the prime minister.

The church is almost empty when I think to look back along our pew, to see that we are the only ones that remain here, inside the stone building, so unfeeling, numbed, and overall—for me— chilled as a meat locker.

Just myself, the prime minster, the archbishop, and the bodyguards.

Without anyone raising a word, the prime minister gets to his feet, and he turns and makes his way along the aisle, headed for the sturdy oak wooden doors which mark the entrance to the church. And my thoughts catch up with my muscles, and I break into activity, following him out, the body guards close at my heels like a pair of subdued bulldogs.

Outside, journalists are packed in behind steel-wire fences, their mouths jabbering long and hard, tablets and microphones jabbing up into the air, and all just rendered as noise. Their breath forms clouds which waft up over their heads, and rises into the chilled late-morning sky.

I keep my step in time with that of the prime minister's, one hand still buried deep in my jacket pocket, ready to pull out the handkerchief if required, if this show of the media scrum causes him to break down and finally show his tenderness to the watching millions.

Or is it billions?

The jet-black car awaits us, and its buffed-up finish reflects the birch trees that tower above us as ghosts in its paintwork, and the sky as a great sheet of chalk, and I glance briefly to the man holding open the door to the backseat of the car, and then I duck down low and follow the prime minister inside.

We ride on along the cobbled road below us, the tyres of the car skipping in and out of the sockets, and occasionally butting the stones. My mouth is dry and my heart is primed as if the chauffeur might be about to drag the car to an abrupt emergency stop. But he continues to drive on, bringing us spiralling downwards, down the hill, away from the church, and back to the pleasant little market town with its hanging baskets and dripping fountain, and the few gawping pensioners with their baskets on wheels, seeming to blossom out of their sleeveless jackets.

At first it is a mere sniffle, an almost unnoticeable shudder of the shoulders. And as I examine the prime minister in profile, I see the twitch of his eyelid and the darkened stubble all over his face become thick with sweat.

I can sense the saltiness burrowing through the air. And it tangs right at the back of my throat. I reach down, for my pocket, for the handkerchief I keep there, and I prepare myself to be at the prime minister's disposal, ready for whatever he feels he must show the world.

And I wait a little longer, feeling the seconds drip by, the tyres of the car slip and slide, in and out of the cobblestones below us, and I glance back out through the rear-view window to the car following behind us . . . to the car which carries the body guards.

Then I look back to the prime minister knowing that we are well and truly alone, and that we sit here, on the backseat of his car, now hidden from the world.

And I watch the tear, that solitary tear, finally escape from the corner of his eye, and roll down his cheek, hang for the briefest of seconds before dripping down onto the front of his suit jacket.

It's as if my whole arm has frozen, but I remind myself of my duty, and produce the handkerchief, hold it out to the prime minister, for him to take.

And he does take it from me.

There is no smile as he brushes the handkerchief along his cheek, wipes the tear away, and then hands the handkerchief back to me without so much as a glance in my direction.

The handkerchief is damp and smells of tears, and I replace it back in the pocket of my suit jacket, and turn towards my own window, my eyes tracing the houses as they pass by us, all those pleasant creams and brightly painted window ledges, and doors. This is a place of cheer, though it'd be difficult to recognise that on a day like today.

A *grey* day.

We ride on, in peace, in silence.

The car scudders to a halt when we reach the road, the path leading to the prime minister's residence. And I glance to him, waiting for my orders, to be told whether or not I might be needed. But all he can manage, in place of looking me in the eye, is a slight shake of his head, and a muttered word I don't have a chance to catch.

He undoes the lock to his door and I listen to the almost imperceptible *creak* as the door opens on its hinge, and then the *crunch* as the sole of his shoe makes contact with the pavement outside.

I wait in the backseat, my breath almost freezing my throat, my mind spinning faster and faster. I face forwards now, knowing instinctively that my role is completed, that I am no longer required.

At least for today.

I concentrate on the chauffeur's headrest, waiting for the *slap* of the closing door, and the *crunch* of the prime minister's footsteps as he heads away, back to the privacy of his residence, away from the glare of the world for a while.

But the sound of the closing door never comes.

When I turn my head, I see the prime minister bent over, leaning into the backseat, towards me. His eyes are skittery, and would be immobile if it wasn't for the shake to them. And his pupils are dilated, and his whole body seems to be shaking. He slumps back down on the backseat, back beside me, and then, without a word, he throws his arms around my neck.

I instantly smell his musky scent, and the slight sour note that carries on his breath, and I feel his warmth pressed up hard against my chest. And I can feel him shuddering, and his sobs sticking in his throat, and the tears rolling down from his eyes, and onto my suit jacket.

I close my eyes and gently surround him with my arms, hoping to offer him some comfort.

Because, on a day like this, what comfort is there to be found?

He mumbles something to me—something I miss—and then he retreats from me, he shuffles his way back along the backseat, still sniffling, not making any sense. And before I know it he's out there, back out on the pavement, and walking fast, back towards the front door of his residence.

My heart skips a beat as I watch on, then the chauffeur says, "Where to, sir?"

The words slither over my tongue, get all unwieldy but I finally grab a hold of them, and reply, "Wait. Wait here," and then shuffle myself along the backseat, and emerge outside the car. Then I call, along the street, to the prime minister as he draws within a couple of steps from his front door. "Uh, sir?"

The prime minister glances in my direction.

I reach into the pocket of my jacket, withdraw the handkerchief, and I hold it between my fingers, flapping a little in the light breeze, and I wait patiently.

Slowly, I watch the prime minister's face transform, his tightly clasped lips give way, just for a moment, and a half-smile cracks his mouth in two. And he strides away from his front door, and approaches me, eyes fixed on the dangling handkerchief. And then, with great delicacy, he untwines it from my fingers.

For the merest fraction of a second, he meets my eye. "Thank you," he says, and then he turns to go.

And I stand there, on the pavement, watching after him, seeing him disappear behind his front door, before I return to the backseat of the car, and instruct the chauffeur to take me home.

To take my back to my studio flat.

Because tomorrow's another day.

MATCH OF THE SEASON: HIS

1

F LOYD UNDERCOAT examined the number on the underside of the folded-up, sun-faded, pink seat, comparing it with the number on his season ticket. He didn't know why he always did this, since the number on his seat—his seat *itself*—was the same for the entire length of the season, but the fact remained that he did.

And, today, after finishing the check of his seat, he unfolded it, feeling the familiar, well-sprung spring somewhere in the inner workings of the thing, and sat down.

It creaked a little under his weight, and he brought his steaming meat-and-potato pie, still tucked neatly into its tinfoil tray, up to his mouth and took a large bite from the crust.

All at once he felt the meat so hot that it almost burned his tongue off, and it did just about the same job on the insides of his cheeks. But he chewed it up, savouring the thick, rich, creamy-smooth gravy there, and he swallowed it down.

When it met with his stomach, the pie sent a shudder through him, and a slight quiver through the pint of ale also in his gut . . . *somewhere* in there . . . and he felt that reassuring, warming sensation flow over him.

Already he could feel this, this . . . *junk* food taking him over, and taking out the taste of his wife's immaculately prepared French toast this morning, and that lemon tea. And with the booming *pop* music which blasted from the Tannoys he could already feel the final strings of the Schubert that had tickled out from the kitchen radio fading away like petals into a blazing furnace.

He had made it. He was at the ground, and on time, and ready to see his boys do their stuff on the football pitch for a solid ninety minutes. And he was away from the wife for a good four—maybe five hours, if he went for a 'quick' pint after the match—and he would return to that unhappy, or should he say, *failing* marriage with a new-found rigor.

Or something like that.

Floyd noticed some motion out of the corner of his eye and, without having to turn round completely, he listened to that *moan* and *creep* of the spring-loaded seat beside him being thrust down, and sat upon.

Odd considering Floyd had spent most of the season with a free seat to either side of him, but, in the end, he'd decided he actually quite liked having the space.

He realised that that was one of the reasons for him coming to these football matches, for being a season ticket holder. Because, to tell the truth, he had never much *liked* football, but the one day it had occurred to him to propose to Gwen, his wife—*not* marriage, although he still shuddered at the day—no, to propose that he start going to the football, to City's home matches every Saturday, she'd seemed to take it as totally normal.

Totally *acceptable*.

And so, here he was, well into his third season, and enjoying his time and space, as much as he was sure that she was enjoying hers back home.

Down on the pitch, the sprinklers were sprinkling, and some children, all of various skin tones and sexes, were pattering back and forth playing on a micro pitch formed of luminescent orange cones. He watched them a few seconds, how all their body movements were exaggerated, and the ball almost comically too large for their dainty little feet.

And then, getting a little bored of this kid-sized spectacle, almost as bored as he got around the sixtieth minute of City's matches—of *any* football match—he passed a casual glance to his newly arrived neighbour.

A silver-haired man, about Floyd's age, and wearing a double-breasted corduroy jacket, buttoned up to his throat in an apparent attempt to ward off the biting winter's afternoon. He had a scarf too, and slightly tanned skin. What, in another life, Floyd might've called *olive*-coloured skin.

The man tilted his head in Floyd's direction.

A slight *gasp* caught at the back of Floyd's throat, and he almost choked on the bite of pie he'd just taken. The potato and meat turned into molten iron and got all piping hot against his tonsils.

He made a few desperate exhales, probably sounding something like a brow-beaten dragon, and then he doubled over, feeling the chunk of pie still lodged in his throat, and making a very good job of choking him.

Next thing Floyd knew he felt an unshaking, mighty pound on his back, between the shoulder blades, a little above where he'd slipped a disk a few years ago, and then he coughed up the pie onto the gritty, grunge-encrusted cement at his feet.

2

FOR A FEW DESPERATE, and intensely embarrassing, seconds he stared at that half-chewed, near-swallowed chunk of meat-and-potato pie and watched the steam rising up off it. And then, as the blood drained back out of his brain, and allowed him to think clearly once more, he undoubled himself, and straightened back up in his seat, panting and sweating profusely.

Remembering himself, he glanced to his side, to his newly arrived neighbour.

And saviour.

Strangely, Floyd felt a slight flutter in his chest, not one for clichés, but he couldn't help remarking that it was something like those butterflies in the stomach regency ladies might have. Yes, just like one of those regency ladies in one of the dozens of nineteenth century novels which lined his study shelves at home.

That *was* odd.

The olive-skinned man sitting beside him was smirking lightly, and now that Floyd got a proper look at him, he saw he had deep, chocolate-toned eyes: rich and exotic, which just about matched his accent, which Floyd pinned as being Italian.

"You are . . . er . . . okay?"

Floyd could hardly think the reply to himself, let alone get the words out through his lips. But he had to try. This man, after all, appeared to have saved his life. Still somewhat flustered, Floyd took another deep breath, feeling it hum right down to the very base of his lungs, and then he said, "Yes, I think I'm quite all right now."

The Italian—?—man gazed at Floyd with those beautiful, chocolate eyes of his, with that warm, seductive smile there, and

Floyd found himself gazing down to the man's lap, to his hands that he clasped there, just below his thigh. The man wore brown *leather* gloves, and these didn't look anything like the ones he might pick up from the discount bin at a service station shop.

No, *these* looked remarkably designer.

As if in acknowledgment of Floyd's stare, the man clasped his hands together, interlocking his fingers, making the leather creak just a little. And then, through his elegant, mahogany lips, he let go of a brief, but sincerely fed-up *sigh*.

"Ah," Floyd began, somewhat unconvincingly, "is something the matter?"

The man continued to face forwards, to look down at the football pitch, to that luscious, extremely well-watered turf that gleamed in the late-afternoon sunlight. He tightened his clasped, leather-gloved hands, and then replied, still facing forwards, "Myself, and my wife, we have just arrived to your city."

"Oh, is that so?"

"Hmm."

Floyd studied the man's reply, not quite sure how to categorise it. It was something between an acknowledgement and a note of surrender. Floyd followed the man's gaze and saw that the kids' game was being broken up by a pair of the track-suited chaperones, and the kids, perhaps because of the thousands of spectators already jammed into their seats, were diligently helping to gather up the luminescent cones and the few spare balls which dotted the turf. Soon the City players would be out on the pitch, and going through their training drills. Then the match would start, and the ninety minutes would play out before them.

Seeing some sort of an entrance point into a discussion, Floyd turned to the man, who made no gesture to move to meet his gaze, and he asked, "Do you like football?"

The man pouted and he arched an eyebrow. "Yes, I like very

much." He shrugged one shoulder, in a way that Floyd knew that if he had tried it he would've looked utterly ridiculous . . . but, then again, he did have those typical—anti-cosmopolitan—male-British genes.

The man continued, "But the British football, I no like as much." And then, without warning, he rammed his shoulder into Floyd's chest, winding him abruptly, and almost sending Floyd doubling over once more.

Only when Floyd glanced up into the man's eyes, did he note the slight smirk there, and that this gesture had been a means to explaining his point.

"Too much physical," the man said.

"Ah," Floyd said, with an uneasy smile back, and taking just about all the self-discipline in the world, all his *British* manners, not to rub at the afflicted spot where the man had shoulder-butted him. "Yes, then I suppose you wouldn't be much of a fan of rugby."

"Rugby?" the man said with his lips pursed as if he might be just a flick of the tongue away from a wolfish spit. "Nah, I do not like the rugby."

Floyd widened his uneasy smile a fraction. "Me neither, too rough and tumble for me." And then he decided that he might push the boat out a bit, just a little. "The, uh, football isn't *really* my idea of good fun either, though, to tell the truth."

Again, the man arched an eyebrow, and Floyd saw that the City players, all track-suited and wearing an assortment of multi-coloured, fluorescent boots, clashing with their light-beige kit, jigged out from the retractable tunnel, and onto the dewy, virgin turf.

Floyd thought that either the man hadn't understood his last statement, or that he'd become distracted by the football players dancing out onto the pitch, by the slight ripple of applause that passed over the supporters in the stands all around him, as if the very act of coming out onto a football pitch *was* something to be applauded.

Then, all of a sudden, and with nostril-flaring, shoulder-squaring, lip-pouting intensity, the man turned full on to Floyd. "In that case," the man said, "why do you *come* to the football?"

FLOYD FELT SOMETHING approaching a daze set in over him. And he caught an aftertaste of that potato-and-meat pie in his mouth, could already feel the skin growing tender where it had burned. Tomorrow, when he woke up, it would be to the feel of dead skin slipping off the inside of his mouth.

Somewhere off in the distance of his consciousness, he heard the crowd break into more clapping, and, looking down to the pitch, Floyd took in Fabian Gentille, the silky-skilled French number nine who, whenever Floyd examined the back page of the local rag, seemed to be the talk of the city. He was clapping his hands above his slickly-oiled, charcoal-shaded hair, and the crowd was responding in kind.

Apparently, according to the local rag, Gentille was City's only hope of avoiding relegation from the first division. Not that Floyd really knew much about the technicalities of all that. But he did know that, more often than not, it was Gentille's name the loud-speaker announcer called out after a goal was scored, attributing the goal to him.

He caught a whiff of the man's cologne, a pungent mix of elder-berries, and something else, something Floyd couldn't put his finger on, but would've liked to have pinned as sandalwood. His wife had a sandalwood perfume back home. Or, at least, what he imagined to have been smelling was sandalwood.

And when Floyd attempted a tentative glance to his side, he noticed that the man was gazing at him intently, those chocolate-brown eyes seeming to drink him in whole, to devour him. It went without saying that Floyd found the gaze of the man just a fraction uncomfortable. And then he remembered that the man had asked *him* a question, and was no doubt anxiously waiting a reply.

That he wanted to know *why* Floyd came to the football.

"I, uh," Floyd began, "well, you see, the thing is that, well, I remember one day just thinking that, you know, perhaps I should do *more* things in the city, that maybe I should get out of the house more."

Already Floyd felt a warm squirming feeling in the pit of his stomach, that strange sense of hundreds of hot worms making their bed there. He had no need to worry about any *real* worms, though, the results of his latest endoscope had come back cleaner than clean. And there should be no reason for the doctor to lie to him.

Should there?

The man elongated his pout, and his other eyebrow joined the first in arching upwards, in making a good offensive on his wrinkled-up forehead, and inching further and further, closer and closer, to that still-thick, silver hair of his.

Much better than the sad little thicket Floyd had to show on his own noggin. But, as he'd learned over the course of his life, some men had much better luck than others.

The man, almost imperceptibly, the motion was so subtle, dabbed his tongue out onto his lower lip, moistening his slightly cracked mahogany lips. "Yes," he said. "Yes, I think that I understand."

Floyd gave him the flash of a nervous grin, and then, feeling those same butterflies flap all about him again, he turned his attention back to the pitch, to Gentille and co as they pranced about, leaping over those things that looked like croquet hoops, then turning round, sprinting back to the start, and doing it all again.

Sport, like many other things, would always be an unfathomable mystery to Floyd. He'd made peace with that fact long ago.

"I have a suggestion," the man said.

"Oh?"

"Yes, uh, why not we go somewhere close, eh? The way that it appears is that not one of us *really* wishes to see the match, and so I am familiar with a place, a *restaurant* nearby, and why not we go there for something to eat. It is of my cuisine, with food from my country."

Floyd scanned this statement, and thought it over to himself. It was odd considering that he—*really*—couldn't care less how today's game turned out for City . . . though, through some sense of ragged regional loyalty, the place that he had chosen to buy his home, he supposed he had some hope City would win, or at least not come off *too* badly. He *had* spent the best part of three seasons watching them, of course.

And he guessed that was where his strange sense of doubt about the man's request came from, since it was through some inner sense of ragged loyalty that he felt like it would be almost impossible for him to tear himself away from the match.

Because, the fact remained, he was something of a completest. He liked to see things through, to have the *whole* set. Back home, in his study, he had every programme from every game for the past two-and-a-bit seasons, all lined up there on his shelf. And he kept his little booklets of season tickets also.

But, sitting here, on this sun-faded, retractable plastic seat, and looking down onto the pitch, he knew, in his heart, that already he had everything he needed to keep up his collections.

If he went with the man, woe betide that he *missed* the actual game, then he would still have those little scraps of—apparently—important paper and glue for his study back home. The day's programme that he had bought earlier. What difference would it really make?

Sure, he wouldn't see twenty-two—if they all behaved them-selves appropriately—professional footballers rushing about on the pitch, getting all red-faced and sweaty for ninety minutes. Nor would he see the prospective goals being scored: the nets bulging, the crowd either crying out in ecstasy or moaning out of disap-pointment, or the players hugging and kissing one another. Once in a while, stripping off their shirts all together, and running, bare-chested, into the delighted crowd . . . only to be flashed a yellow card by the referee when they returned.

True, he would miss all that.

But his collection would remain unharmed, in fact it would be *enhanced* with his crisp day's programme he had carefully rolled up in the inside pocket of his jacket, lightly prodding him in the ribs at that exact moment, and he would have his season ticket duly stamped, and voided.

In fact, he would be *much better off* going with this man, to this *restaurant* he suggested. Surely that would be a memory to cherish, rather than one that would quickly fade from his mind, as the one of this forthcoming football match would.

Decided, he turned to face the man full-on. And, strange that he didn't notice till he was actually speaking, with his gleaming tone of voice, that he was grinning from ear to ear. "Yes, that sounds like a marvellous idea. Is it an Italian restaurant?"

The man scowled, narrowed his eyes till Floyd could only see the sheen of his eyeballs between his eyelashes. "No, it is not *Italian*. It is Hungarian . . ."

"Oh, Hungarian, you are *Hungarian?*"

"Yes," the—apparently Hungarian—man said, "I am of Hungary."

With a final glance down at the pitch, and with something of an apologetic half-smile at Gentille, who, of course, was one-hundred-per-cent focused on leaping those croquet hoops, and not at all interested in Floyd, they both stood back up and weaved their way back along the empty row, and out of the stadium.

4

T HE RESTAURANT was located down a back alley in the centre of town. This was a locale that Floyd was not familiar with. He had lived in the city for about ten years now, where he'd seen out the last years of his career.

Secretly Floyd had always wanted to retire to some seaside village somewhere, but he knew his wife would never have any of it. She enjoyed being in the centre of a bustling metropolis, and though they almost never went out *anywhere*, she almost always intoned about not being able to go out to the theatre, or to a museum, or an art gallery on a whim.

And so, he supposed, that was why he'd eked out that tiny little niche, that season-ticket seat of his at the football, somewhere he could go for a little peace and quiet, away from all the hustle and bustle of the city . . . even if that place *was* in the middle of lunking brutes and expletive-filled chants.

When they entered the restaurant, the *Hungarian* man nodded to the man Floyd supposed to be the headwaiter of the establishment. He had light-brown hair, though the slicked-down gel spread through his hair did a good job of making it seem almost black.

The headwaiter zig-zagged through the packed-together tables, with their pristine white tablecloths, and, with a muttered word to the Hungarian man, in what Floyd could only assume to be Hungarian, the headwaiter dropped a pair of burgundy-colour, leather-bound menus on the table and then pattered back off.

For just a few moments, Floyd absorbed the bedlam all around him. His eyes darted between all the tables, seemingly every chair occupied in the place, and to the multicultural—or were they all Hungarian?—clientele.

The language—*languages?*—in the air was thick and opaque,

and, only when Floyd had moved on from that detail, did he notice the open-plan kitchen, the narrow window which looked into the steaming, smoking kitchens nestled deeper into the restaurant, and those heavenly smells came to overwhelm him.

And—goodness!—was it a collection of smells.

Garlic.

Thyme.

Rosemary.

And a bunch of other herbs and spices he would've had a hard time naming. He wasn't much of a foodie, let alone a chef himself. While he could appreciate the finer tastes, the richer sauces, etcetera, he never brought his mind to *studying* such matters.

He recalled some rather vulgar Saturday night television comic putting it bluntly when he'd said that 'it all comes out the same the other end'. And while he couldn't quite bring himself to agree with the wording, he did agree with the sentiment.

Already, and despite that pie back at the stadium, Floyd felt his mouth begin to water and his stomach rumble as he took in the plates laid before the other diners. He looked at how most . . . no, *all*, of the diners were male here. And how they all tucked their napkins into their shirt collars.

Floyd smiled pleasantly in the Hungarian man's direction, and decided that, now, following that almost totally mute journey from the stadium to the restaurant, this might be an appropriate time to ask him his name. And so he did.

"Chah-bah," the Hungarian man said.

"Pardon?"

"Chah-bah."

"Uh, how do you, erm, . . ."

"Spell like See, uh, Ess, uh, Ay, Bee, Ay. Chah-bah."

"Ah," Floyd said, thinking this over, and trying to get it straight in his head.

Finally he did.

Csaba.

Yes, that was right.

"Mine's Floyd," Floyd said.

Csaba mouthed Floyd's name a couple of times, as if practising, and then he spoke it out loud. "Fel-oyd?"

"No, no, *Floyd*."

"Fel-oyd?"

"*Floyd*."

Csaba squinted at Floyd, as if trying to unravel some mystery about him, and then he turned his attention to the menu lying on the table before him, and snatched it up, flipping through the pages.

With nothing else to say, Floyd plucked up his menu, and unfolded it. Like most restaurant menus that Floyd had run into in the course of his life, this one had something sticky inside it, and it made a slight squelching sound as he opened it. That wasn't what unnerved him, however, what did though, was when he leafed through the laminated pages and discovered that it was all in a foreign language—*Hungarian?*

And so, he promptly glanced up over his menu, and met Csaba's eye with his own, almost losing the question on his lips in those deep, chocolate eyes of his.

Csaba smiled wryly, those mahogany lips pouting again, just a little. "I order something for you, yes? Something nice."

Only when Floyd glanced about did he notice the headwaiter—or as Floyd had established in the past few minutes, the *only* waiter in the place—had sprung up at his elbow, and was standing, slightly slouched, an unlit cigarette dangling from his lips, and looking dopey-eyed at Csaba. He didn't have a notepad, or even a pen for that matter.

Csaba rattled off something that, as far as Floyd might have known, could have been rat poison, and then the headwaiter shrugged back off across the restaurant, leaving the two of them alone once more.

Csaba's next gesture rather confused Floyd, as Csaba reached across the table, to one of Floyd's hands gripping tight to the table-cloth—the *left* hand—and laid his own knobbly, and yet soft-skinned, fingers over Floyd's. He spoke in a raspy, almost too-quiet voice. "Now tell me, Fel-oyd, do you have wife?"

Floyd felt his stomach dip long and hard, as he found himself saying, "Yes, yes, I do. Why do you ask?"

"Bee-cos," Csaba said, "I too have a *wife.*"

Floyd glanced back down, to Csaba's fingers gripping his own, and he admired their handsomeness, how it appeared that Csaba had truly taken good care of his hands . . . unlike how Floyd had treated his own, never bothering to moisturise or any of that nonsense. And yet, now, it struck him as odd that he should notice the condition of another man's hands, let alone compare them to his own body-care routines.

Floyd had something on the tip of his tongue, some snappy response to feedback to Csaba, some quip that, most likely thinking it over a second time, would've got all lost in translation, when he heard the *thud* of a pair of soup bowls landing on the table before them, courtesy of the surly waiter.

5

FLOYD was glad of the interruption, pleased to see that he could now take up his soup spoon, and suckle away at this greasy, yet fine-smelling, broth before him, and think things over for a while.

Csaba had now taken his hand back, and had lowered his head to his soup bowl in way that reminded Floyd of a thoroughbred horse drinking from a trough.

An *extremely* thoroughbred horse.

Floyd absorbed that mounted, buttery grease, and he felt himself warm from the inside out. He thought about how long it had been since he'd had truly *hearty* food, food for the soul, as they said.

Too long, he supposed.

Everything these days, everything *Gwen* prepared, seemed to be stuck up its own arse within an inch of its life, namely that it all seemed to have some French flourish to its name, and, if not that, then it often had a sprinkle of seeds of some sort, or some expensive-looking and finely whipped cream of some other.

Yes, this soup was a good thing. And, only having sucked up most of the goodness, having got down to that last, thin puddle at the bottom of the bowl, did he remind himself that the whole salvation of the soup's arrival—it coming just when it did—had been that he could think things over, find a suitable way to respond to that odd remark of Csaba's.

Now, though, he was coming to the end of the soup, and his mind was still just as blank as it had been before.

He was on the point of blabbing out something or other when, with that gradual *scuff* of shoes over the well-worn restaurant carpet, he noticed his old friend the headwaiter returning once more.

This time with a bottle of red wine precariously held under one arm, and a pair of plates in his hands, steaming hard and fast, both plates stuffed full of *food*.

6

I T WAS AFTER this second mercy, and two glasses of wine, that Floyd eventually managed to formulate some scrap of conversation to throw out at Csaba. And he almost stopped himself cold before he had even started, already doubting himself, and his intent. But, before he could end it entirely, he got the words past his lips.

"Uh, you said you have a wife?"

Csaba yanked his napkin from his shirt collar and dabbed at his lips, turned an even deeper shade of mahogany from the red wine. He gently laid the napkin down on the table, beside his plate, now picked clean. "Yes," he said.

Floyd waited for something more, for another response to come. But, it seemed, none was forthcoming. And so he did what seemed to be the only polite thing.

He slipped into silence.

Of course, that response could mean all manner of things. It might be that his companion was separated from his wife, or even divorced, and perhaps hadn't quite shaken the habit of calling her his 'wife'. And, considering the little Floyd knew about Hungarian customs, and coupling that with Csaba's rudimentary knowledge of the English language, he supposed it better to avoid awkwardness as well as he could.

She might even be *dead*.

Before Floyd had to scour his brains too hard to find something else to say, Csaba beat him to it.

"Do you living far from here?" Csaba said.

A little stunned at the question, Floyd replied, "Not too far," and then, managing to drop just a little of his well-cushioned manners, added, "Why?"

Csaba shrugged, gave a hard pout, and then said, "Because I

would like to know your house." He continued to face forwards, looking off into the restaurant, almost as if he wasn't aware Floyd was looking at him intently. "My wife," Csaba continued, "she is lonely and would like a friend."

"Is that so?"

"Yes."

Floyd thought this over to himself, studied it from all angles. What exactly was the intent of Csaba? Was this all some clumsy-handed attempt at making friends? He wondered, and thought that he was someone to talk about clumsiness, when he was just about the most awkward soul to walk the Earth.

But still, he couldn't quite get his head around the request. And so he decided to do something which made him deeply and horribly uncomfortable. He decided to think out loud.

"My wife," Floyd said, "well, the thing is that she's rather, uh, how should I put this . . . yes, right, she likes to have space for herself, you see? She likes to be on her own often. The thing is, well, she doesn't *have* many friends. Doesn't *like* to have friends, really, truth be told."

Csaba kept up his stern pout, his lips still tightly sealed.

Floyd stared hard at him, waiting for his reply, wondering if he'd understood everything he'd just said . . . all the nuances he'd muckily attempted to communicate.

And then Csaba burst into life. But it wasn't in Floyd's direction, it was with a flurry of a wave to the waiter, who stood over on the other side of the restaurant.

Floyd watched on as the waiter bobbed through the other diners and up to their table, and he slapped a piece of paper with scrawled biro on it face-down onto the table cloth. Only a few seconds later, when Csaba had already slid the paper towards himself, did Floyd realise that it was the bill, and that he had made no offer to pay for it.

Floyd flapped his lips, perhaps with a touch less futility than a banked fish, because Csaba cut him off immediately.

"I pay," Csaba said. "I invite. My *invitation*." Then, after he'd dug out a pair of crisp, new, twenty pound notes and set them down on the tablecloth with the *thud* of his palm, he caught Floyd's eye sharply. "We go to your house. You show me your house."

Floyd just continued to stare at the receipt there, the pair of twenty pound notes now nestled beneath the paper, and he couldn't help wondering if—*really*—he might've been much better off staying to see the City match.

7

J UST AS HE NORMALLY DID, Floyd took the bus. For some reason he expected that Csaba might refuse and demand they take a taxi, and the truth was, most winter days, like this one, with that real kicking chill in the air, Floyd would take one. There was no getting over the fact that he was getting older—*plumper*— and that in his worsening condition he could hardly afford a slip on some ice, a fall onto a shin-high brick wall.

It might finish him off.

But something at the back of Floyd's mind told him that he wanted to take public transport right now, that even with the night draping itself over the backside of the city, where they were right now, he wished to take the bus.

Something about the bus was soothing. Maybe its gentle, woozy engine *hum*, or the dusty scent of the seats, or maybe even that sharp tang of disinfectant that seemed to hang around, *stick* to the floors of the bus, holding on just as tight as the dried-up, gobbed-out scraps of chewing gum.

And so they took the bus.

They took up a seat on the lower deck, the seats just behind the driver, so that Floyd could see himself, and Csaba sat beside him, in three different mirrors. He wasn't sure *why* he found that reassuring exactly, but he did. He liked having those mirrors about him.

They rode through the packed city, Saturday night grinding slowly into action, and past the streams of people—*young* people— queuing up to get into bars and clubs. The women—and he could never quite believe *how*—all wore those impossibly skimpy dresses, and the boys just their shirts, if not short-sleeved then with the long-sleeves rolled all the way up to the elbow.

Things had been very different when *he'd* been a youth, that was for certain.

The bus barrelled along the quicker stretches of the city streets, and at this time it wasn't all that hectic getting *out* of the city. And, glancing at his watch, Floyd saw that the match hadn't quite finished yet, so they wouldn't have to contend with the football traffic on their way back out to the suburbs where he lived.

After another twenty minutes or so of the thickest of thick silences Floyd had ever experienced, the bus turned the corner and the stop nearest Floyd's home drew into sight. For some inexplicable reason he felt a spark in his stomach, as if he might be home safe, *almost* there, *almost* back.

And so when he turned to look at Csaba, he did so with a smile splitting his cheeks. "This is it," Floyd said. "We're here."

"Hmm."

Floyd nodded a couple of times, still grinning like an idiot, and then the two of them got to their feet. Floyd rang the Stop bell and the bus slowly hummed to a halt at the stop.

8

A GROUP OF YOUTHS, all dressed in tracksuits, one of them straddling a bike, all hung about the bus stop. Clouds of smoke puffed up into the air, and Floyd quickly identified the sickly sweet scent of marijuana. And he hustled off along the pavement, already feeling Csaba on his heels, following him on the way.

They got away from the youths scot-free, or so it seemed. At least Floyd didn't absorb any shoutings-out after them, or any directed spitting.

Floyd's street was deserted. All the cars parked up, most of them half up onto the curb. Lights glowed out from within curtained-off front rooms and he could hear the light *babble* of television racket worming its way out from inside several of the homes.

He glanced back, saw Csaba following him still, maybe two or three paces behind, and, almost subconsciously, he quickened his pace, made his way for his house.

For good-old number seventy-one.

He came to a stop when he reached the pinewood front gate, the one that he'd hung there himself. One of his few forays into DIY, and perhaps one of his last, considering the density of swearing and the two screwdrivers he'd gone through to achieve it.

Gwen had made him promise that.

He settled his hand on top of the gate, and couldn't shake the feeling of what he must do now, and that which he *really* and *sincerely* didn't want to do. But he was a polite man, and what was more, this kindly foreign gentleman had bought him lunch . . . and a *late* lunch at that.

So, feeling that odd itching sensation in his chest, he got the question out there between them. "Uh, would you like to come in for cup of tea?"

Csaba, though, was casting his gaze over the façade of Floyd's house . . . well, that was one way of putting it, another might be to say that he was *devouring* it with his gaze, taking the whole thing in with great big gulps.

He shot Floyd a sidelong glance, and Floyd saw the glimmering of the streetlight in those round, beautiful, almost tree-bark-like, eyes. "You are good to me," Csaba said. "Very polite."

"Yes, well," Floyd said, feeling the warmth in his cheeks grow, and realising that he was blushing, perhaps from the rawness of the words, "I . . . well, really, I should be the one that's thanking you, for such a slap-up meal. And you should, uh, come inside for a cup of tea, to meet my wife."

"Hmm," Csaba replied.

Floyd felt that itchy sensation break out over the entire surface of his skin, and his heart well up in his throat. This whole situation was so awkward, so *odd*, and he thought to himself that he would give anything—*anything at all*—to be extricated from it.

Before he could repeat his invitation, Csaba took him quite off guard, as he swooped down, from his height, which Floyd only now really seemed to register as *towering* and planted a dry and woozy kiss on his lips.

Floyd gripped the pine gate between his fingers, and felt half a dozen splinters embed themselves there, in his skin. Floyd's voice came slowly, and thickly, from the depths of his throat. "Ahh!" he said, responding to the pain, though the pain was the least of his worries.

Csaba held his lips to Floyd's another moment, and then Floyd felt the warm scrub of Csaba's beard retreat from his own, less-hairy, face. Csaba regarded Floyd silently, in the half-light of the streetlights, and Floyd really had no idea what to say next.

But the words, this time, for once, did seem to come. "I, uh, thank you ever so much for the dinner, really, it was *lovely*."

And, at the same time, he managed to unlatch the garden gate from the other side—a small miracle seeing as he usually had to swoop his neck over the damn gate and look at the catch while he somehow tried to fathom it.

Now standing on the other side of the gate, he quietly met Csaba's eye, and managed a sheepish grin at him. "Uh, yes, so I suppose, maybe, I shall see you . . . uh, at the football? Yes, at the football?"

Csaba just remained totally silent, a lumbering presence there in the twilight gloom.

Floyd managed another twitching grin and then bobbed his way along the garden path and up to his front door. He fumbled in his pocket for his keys and then—again on some clumsy lucky streak—found the right one straight away and shoved it into the keyhole, listening for that familiar, homey, mechanical *scrub* as it went in.

With a fresh smile, and with one foot half over the doormat, Floyd glanced back over his shoulder and thanked Csaba another dozen times.

Csaba just stood there, in the same place as before, staring after him.

Dialling down to a sheepish, apologetic grin, Floyd finally shut the door behind him, with a gentle *whoomph* of night air seething round the gap and soon dissipated by the warmth from the central heating in the front hall.

And Floyd stood there, in the front hall, among the dank-smelling coats and shoes that were all tumbled about on the tiled floor, and then he pressed his back up against the front door, felt his heart pounding in his chest.

From the kitchen he could hear the *snap* and *crackles* of cooking, of Gwen there, rustling up his tea. And he thought, in a dazed state, he had only just had his lunch. His stomach was still very much full. Almost to tipping point.

As he finally prised himself off the door, and heard his wife's nasal tone winding its way along the corridor, out from the kitchen, he chanced a final glance through the peephole on the front door.

He looked to the garden gate, and to the street outside his house. And he was certain to check twice, to make double sure, that the hulking figure of Csaba was gone. That he'd shifted off into the night. Perhaps back off up the road to catch another bus, or to get a taxi.

To return to his wife.

Just as Floyd must, now, return to his.

MATCH OF THE SEASON: HERS

1

G WEN UNDERCOAT slaved away in the heat of the stove. She felt the beads of sweat tickling their way down her back, pooling there at the base of her blouse and dampening the fabric. The steam rushed up her nostrils and she caught a heady whiff of garlic, and onions—God, how she'd always hated onions.

Tears gathered in her eyes and she wiped them away with the sleeve of her blouse, feeling the slight scrub of the material against her delicate skin. The skin she'd spent a fortune on maintaining in terms of moisturisers, softeners and tautners. It never seemed all that logical to her, but she'd done it all the same.

At least it seemed just about what every other woman did.

The onions and garlic crackled in the frying pan, leaping about in the boiling-hot olive oil there, and she could already feel those first hunger pangs striking her. And then, over her shoulder, she heard those slightly muffled footsteps coming down the stairs, the creaking of the floorboards.

She tossed the onions and garlic round in the base of the frying pan and wiped away another layer of sweat from her forehead. At this rate she'd have to stick in a whole basket of blouses into the washing machine before she even got round to eating.

"Dear?"

Gwen had no need to turn round, to look away from her cooking, she knew just who it was behind her, looming in the doorway to the kitchen.

Her husband, Floyd.

She had seen him almost every day of their thirty-six years of marriage . . . which wasn't to count their 'courtship' which lasted another four *long* years . . . and so she really had no need of seeing that fairly bloated, puce face there, stuffed into the neck of an anorak.

She whipped up her spatula and tossed the garlic and onions round in the oil, and then, on a whim, she reached for the pot of pepper sitting beside the stove and tossed in a good lashing.

Sometimes life was for the living, what could she say?

She was already eyeing the salt pot when she responded over her shoulder, still facing the stove, "Off to the football, are you?"

"Yes, dear," he replied.

"Back for dinner?"

"I expect so, but . . ."

She waited for him to complete the sentence, but nothing followed. Truth be told she'd had something on her mind for weeks now . . . for quite a while. It had all started one day, about three years ago now, when Floyd had decided that he wanted to go to football matches.

She had seen it at once for what it was.

She knew him too well not to see right through it. From his point of view she could see that he felt like being here, being in the house the whole week, now the two of them were retired, meant him getting under her feet, here and there.

Floyd spent most of the week shuttered off in his study, keeping out of her way, and she found that somewhat endearing . . . if not a little infuriating. Because, if he really *did* have a problem living with her, then why didn't he just come out and say it?

But that was asking a lot of a man, she supposed.

The last few weeks, though, that was what she'd grown more concerned about. Whereas before Floyd would return maybe an hour—an hour and a half—after the football had finished, now he'd caught onto the habit of disappearing off till the early evening.

Not coming home until seven or eight o'clock. Not that she minded, of course, he was free to do whatever he wanted now he was retired, and she wasn't likely to become the wife to be looked upon as the old 'ball and chain'.

Still, she did wonder.

The way he came back in after the football, all jolly and every-thing, that was what had started her mind off spinning, made her think deeper on this whole thing. Begin to *suspect* another woman involved.

She *did* snatch up a pinch of salt and chuck that over the oil and garlic and onion, and she watched it spit up a few fumes in protest. She really loved cooking, it was the one thing she could really retreat into, slip into. The feeling was almost elemental, what with the zingy tastes, the full flavours, and that satisfying warming feeling deep down in her gut after a long-sought *filling* dinner. She wasn't cooking for Floyd, no, he would be off to the football shortly. She was merely making herself something tasty for a Saturday lunch at home.

All alone.

She waited to see if Floyd was going to add anything further, if he was going to fill in that silence that he'd spun out into the kitchen. But it didn't seem likely. Typical of *that* man to clam up whenever he had anything really worth saying—something that didn't have to do with a clue to the newspaper crossword puzzle.

"See you later, then?" Floyd finally added.

Gwen turned to her chopping board, took in the breast of chicken she'd spent much of the last ten minutes slicing into cube-shaped pieces, and then said, "Yes, I'll see you later."

2

I T WAS just after she'd dropped the diced-up chicken pieces into the frying pan, got them sizzling around with the oil and the garlic and the onions that she, inexplicably, began to tear up.

At first she was sure that it was the onions that had done it, and maybe she'd overdone it a little with the pepper, but she knew that wasn't the case more or less right away when she felt her shoulders heaving and the sobs coming right from the base of her chest.

She blinked as many of the tears from her eyes as she could, and tried to go on cooking, but it was impossible. She simply couldn't cook like this. *Feeling* like this.

And so she left the chicken bubbling away in its oil, and left behind the pleasant . . . no, the *wonderful* scents of her cooking, to go off into the downstairs toilet and gorge herself with toilet roll.

After a good few blows, she felt almost all right again. It felt good sometimes to get all that built-up snot out. To have a good cry. And yet, at the back of her mind, she felt that nagging old feeling that . . . *emptiness* there, that indefinable feeling of emptiness within her, and she knew that she was a long way from solving her problem.

From solving this problem with Floyd.

She sat down on the folded-down toilet seat and stared at herself in the circular, oak-framed mirror hung opposite her on the wall.

Old.

That was what looked back at her.

Wrinkles. Mottled cheeks. Sunken eye sockets.

Was it any wonder he didn't *want* her anymore?

At their age was anyone *meant* to want her anymore?

She felt a lump form in her throat and she swallowed it down.

She tried to bury herself in those scents drifting through the house from the kitchen. The rich taste of the chicken. The herbs all there hanging in the air. But . . . but, this time she knew that pure sensory overload just wouldn't work. That she needed, really needed—

The doorbell rang.

A shudder ran up Gwen's spine, as it always did when the doorbell rang. Same thing with the telephone. She had no real idea why. She wasn't a criminal, not a crook or anything like that. In fact, looking back on her life, there wasn't even one thing she could put her finger on, that she could identify, herself having affected for either good or ill.

Was that something to be proud of?

The doorbell rang again, the porcelain bells strung up in the front hall and tuned to a sombre D minor jangled again.

That had been one of Floyd's much-maligned DIY projects. That one had taken almost as much swearing as the hanging of the garden gate. But the doorbell *did* make a pretty sound, she had to admit that much.

Still, it didn't matter how pretty the sound, because the very fact of what that sound represented, someone at the door, *someone* invading on her personal space, turned her insides out.

Just as with the telephone, the one which had that vintage phone box ring to it, and should've been pleasant—uninvasive.

And, yet, the very *idea* put her on edge.

And she always felt compelled to answer.

She remembered once, back when she'd been a young girl, no older than nine or ten years old, and she'd heard the doorbell ring. When she'd gone to answer it a flustered, middle-aged man wearing a trilby and suit jacket had been on the doorstep. She remembered his thin-framed glasses and how he'd smelled of cinnamon . . . that was one thing with cooking, it had given her a whole catalogue of fragrances to draw on . . . and he'd gone all wide-eyed, and reached out, grabbed hold of her shoulder and demanded to know if her parents were at home.

Gwen had shaken her head, told him that her parents were out. Then the man had asked to use the house telephone, because there had been an accident. Of course, half in shock, Gwen had stepped aside, allowed the man to slip in past her, into the house. And while he'd used the phone, barked away at the police or ambulance, she'd stepped out over the doorstep and glanced out into the road.

Two cars, she remembered them quite clearly. One, a Morris Minor, the other some sleek-looking car that she'd never have been able to identify, but she knew enough, even then, as a young girl, to know it was expensive.

And she recalled how the Morris Minor had been half-destroyed, its bonnet bent up at a forty-five degree angle, and the sleek-looking car apparently having just ploughed right into it.

And then she'd seen the woman, the woman's *face*, gazing out at her from beneath the windscreen, with that dazed expression, and a trickle of blood rolling down from her temple. Next thing Gwen had known, the man had thanked her and then swept back out to the roadside, to see to the scene of the accident.

After that Gwen had gone back inside, gone upstairs to her room to play with her dolls. And when her parents had got back home, and they'd seen all the kafuffle with the police outside, they'd asked her what had happened, and she really hadn't been able to tell them anything . . . because, really, she'd seen nothing.

Later that evening, she remembered sitting at the top of the stairs, as she often did while she waited for her mother to bring up her bedtime glass of milk, and how she'd overheard her father speaking on the phone, and when he'd hung up the phone he'd told Gwen's mother that the woman was doing fine, that she was going to be fine.

And, ever since that day, even though Gwen really knew that

there had been dozens of other houses on their street, dozens of other neighbours to lend a phone to call the emergency services, she had always made a point of answering every phone and every doorbell she could.

As far as she knew there might be a life on the line. A life that needed saving.

The doorbell rang out again, and Gwen shifted herself off the lid of the toilet. She sniffed a couple of times, and decided she didn't have time to blow her nose again as she stomped out into the front hall, and, with a final, deep and cleansing breath, she undid the latch and opened up.

3

THERE, on the doorstep, stood a prim, grey-haired woman, about Gwen's age, at least by her guessing. She was well made-up, enough so as to keep her wrinkles at bay and to bring out the luminescence of her almost . . . *purple* eyes. She had olive-toned skin and pert, neat, nearly mauve lips. She fluttered her eyelashes, once, twice, before she spoke.

"You Mrs Undercoat?"

Gwen felt a daze wash over herself, but she couldn't think of anything else to say other than, "Yes."

"May I come in?"

Gwen held back there, standing on the doorstep. She caught a whiff of the woman's perfume: lilies, a slight sweet dash of something else too . . . strawberries? The scent sent her deeper into her daze and she felt her mind becoming all woozy, perhaps a migraine coming at her from some previously unseen nook of her cranium.

"Uh, who, I mean, who are *you?*" Gwen found herself saying.

The woman pursed her lips, arched her shoulders, and then said, "My name is Margit."

"Margit?" Gwen said, still feeling like her words were distant and floaty.

"Yes. May I come in?"

In that moment, Gwen sniffed out the smell of burning, carrying right over her shoulder. She remembered the lunch. The chicken she'd been cooking up, and she turned on her heel and dashed back into the house, without so much as another word to the woman.

Back at the stove, Gwen snatched up her spatula and went at the chicken which was now making a good job of burning itself onto the base of the frying pan. And these were supposed to be non-stick. But, then again, she guessed these kinds of frying pans needed a bare minimum of culinary supervision.

Gwen snatched up the bottle of olive oil standing beside her elbow and flipped off the lid. Then she scattered the oil over the chicken and watched the oil steam up in little puffs of cloud. And the chicken simmered down, stopped burning itself so badly to the base of the frying pan.

"Your house is quite lovely."

Gwen's heart bounced up into her throat, and she felt it pound away there. She spun round and looked off behind her. She wasn't sure quite what she had expected, she had recognised the voice at once, of course, and she'd already identified it as belonging to the woman who'd come to the door. But seeing the woman, standing here in her kitchen now, staring right into those odd purply eyes, she felt a shudder run up her spine.

What did this woman want? Did she have no sense of manners?

Before Gwen parted her lips to deliver either shriek or stark reprimand, she thought it over another second. What if this woman was some mental deficient? Maybe she'd wandered out of some care home or other and managed to waddle her way along the street—along *Gwen's* street—and for some bonkers reason decided to ring the doorbell?

Gwen had to take care. Not least because bonkers people could be truly dangerous.

And so, instead of screaming, or something, she met the woman's eyes with a level gaze, and managed a fledgling smile. "Erm, are you lost?"

The woman—Margit—cocked her head slightly to one side. For the first time Gwen could really take in the woman's stature. She was about a head shorter than Gwen, and so standing about five-five, something like that. And, although it was something which Gwen didn't often notice, she saw that the woman had a large pair of breasts. *That* was mostly prevalent because the woman wore a low-necked jumper showing off her cleavage.

Which, much to Gwen's surprise, really wasn't all that wrinkled.

The woman blinked a couple more times.

Gwen had noticed that the woman had an accent earlier, a *foreign* accent, and so she wondered if the woman had understood her at all. She was right on the cusp of repeating what she'd said when the woman finally broke in.

The woman sighed heavily, her shoulder rising and falling with great drama, and her eyes widening and nostrils flaring with the apparent effort. "I have come about my *hus*-band."

"Oh?" Gwen said, feeling a slight pang at the base of her stomach, and already eyeing the cordless phone which hung from its wall charger just a few paces from where the woman stood.

If this woman pulled a knife, or whatever, then she would simply have to run the gauntlet, dash right over to the phone, snap it up and rapidly pound out the number for the emergency services.

Or should she just try to escape?

From where Gwen stood, at the stove, her only way out of the kitchen depended on her successfully negotiating the woman, either going round her, or, as Gwen thought with a lump forming in her throat, going *over* her.

But the woman, at least for the time being, didn't seem to be aggressive. She kept up an easy, slightly weary smile, and, for someone who had effectively burgled their way into someone else's house, a fairly confident demeanour.

Gwen thought back to the woman's question, and realised that she'd left it hanging. Or had it been a question at all, or just a statement?

. . . A command?

"You're looking for your husband?"

The woman clasped her eyes shut and shook her head. Then she pressed a hand to her temple, and Gwen saw the multitude of rings there, all golden, silver, some rubies—a diamond or two?—and then, and this took Gwen totally off guard, a tear rolled down the woman's cheek.

4

FOR SOME REASON, that was the first time during their encounter that Gwen felt any urge to rush into any sort of action. She listened to soles of her house shoes, the flat plimsolls, slap against the tiles of the kitchen floor as she tiptoed over to the woman. And, before she knew it, she was throwing her arms about the woman, squeezing her to her chest.

Only when Gwen pressed her face into the woman's hair did she realise that she was crying too, and that her own tears were falling onto the woman's scalp. When she attempted to wrench herself loose, the woman held onto her strongly, in a childlike way. And who was Gwen to pull herself away? This woman was obviously in a real state.

Was *Gwen* in such a state too?

They remained like that for what seemed like hours. When Gwen finally got herself loose it was to go over and check on the frying chicken again, and to add the ingredients required for the sauce.

In the meantime, when Gwen glanced back over her shoulder to the woman, she saw that she'd produced a make-up mirror and that she was inspecting herself, dabbing at the smudged make-up around her eyes, unclumping eyelashes, and splodging anything that needed splodging.

Thinking quickly, Gwen spied the box of tissues standing over on the kitchen counter, and she trudged over to it, whipped out a fair handful and then passed them over to the woman. Then, with infinite patience, a patience she'd never really felt in her life before —at least when it came to Floyd—she waited for the woman to speak to her.

The woman dabbed away the makeup she didn't wish to salvage, and then handed the sooty-stained tissue over to Gwen,

180

making a slightly pouty grin. The woman's cheeks had puffed out from her crying and her eyelids too had gone all bloated. But, through it all, the woman opened up into a wider grin.

A winning grin.

And she showed off several rows of immaculately preserved, pearl-white teeth, and the hint of a velvety smooth tongue. "Thanks to you," she said.

"You're welcome," Gwen said, smiling back, already feeling a strange, unplaceable affinity with this woman.

The woman looked beyond Gwen, to the stove behind her, to the food steaming away there, to the chicken cooking. Just looking into her eyes, seeing that glassy reflection of her eyeballs, Gwen knew that the woman had done a fair amount of mindless wandering today. And so, Gwen supposed, had she.

With an ever-growing smile, Gwen turned to the woman and said, "Would you like to join me for a spot of lunch?"

"Yes, would be lover-ly," the woman replied.

5

S O, the two of them sat down to lunch, splitting the chicken between the two of them, with some slices of wholemeal toast—made from the bread Gwen had baked earlier that morning, while Floyd had still been snoring away upstairs in bed—and they ate in silence, only the clinking of the cutlery on the porcelain plates disrupting it.

They had a glass of white wine each too. That had been an impulse. As a rule Gwen never drank in the middle of the day— some New Year's resolution she'd made long ago, so many years ago she'd forgotten what the year had been.

But this was a special occasion. And, if Floyd was off having his fun, whatever that might exactly be, then why shouldn't she have *hers?*

With a full stomach and a head full of wine, Gwen found the strangeness of the situation ebbing away into a woozy and pleasant fog. In fact, this seemed like just about the most natural thing in the world. What could be more pleasant? Sat here at lunch with a perfect stranger, a stranger to share the meal she'd lovingly spent the best part of the morning preparing.

Their plates were empty now, before them, and Gwen studied the woman sitting opposite her as she knotted her napkin and dabbed at her lips with it. When she brought the napkin back down, dropped it in a screwed-up ball at the side of her plate, she glanced up at Gwen, seeming to take great care in meeting her eye, as if she might break something with a sharp glare. The woman smiled, somewhat sheepishly. "I want to talk with you, since before today."

"Oh?" Gwen said, feeling the woozy sensation of the alcohol working at her mind, stripping it of its sharpness.

"Yes, I have."

Again, losing her inhibitions, Gwen continued, "I'm sorry, but have we met before? If we have, I'm afraid that I must admit to not remembering our meeting. So please excuse me for sounding terribly rude. Some people are good with faces and terrible with names, but, to be honest, I've always been quite awful with both."

The woman's eyes flickered over Gwen's for several seconds, and Gwen could almost imagine those cogs turning inside her skull, of her sorting and switching, of her analysing her words and translating them into her own language.

It wasn't that the woman hadn't understood her before, Gwen saw that now. It was that the woman needed some time to put the pieces of the jigsaw puzzle together, to get everything straight in her mind before she spoke.

And Gwen gave her the time.

The woman clasped her hands in her lap, out of sight to Gwen, blocked by the sturdy, oak dining table between them, and she spoke with a weak, almost inaudible voice. "No," she said. "We have not never met one another."

Gwen glanced to her wine glass, saw the little puddle remaining, and then she looked to the bottle, still about half full. She reached across the table, taking hold of the still-chilled bottle and poured it out into her glass, listening to the *glug-glug* as the wine emerged and then splashed up against the side of the wine glass.

The woman continued, "But there is a reason for me to come to see you today." She paused a moment, glanced up, meeting Gwen's eye for the most fleeting of seconds, and then added, "I want come when your husband not home."

Even through the alcoholic haze, and the fresh wine swilling down through her, warming her as it went, she felt that sharp, cool pang in the pit of her gut, and her muscles all seemed to squeeze up.

Every nerve in her body tautened.

But Gwen managed to keep her voice level, even-handed. "Why

didn't you want to come and see me when my husband wasn't home?"

The woman ceased playing with her hands beneath Gwen's line of sight, and brought them back up onto the table. She laid her hands down on the tablecloth, palms flat, and stared at them as if they were something apart from her. Some appendage she had no control over. "You see," she began, "your *hus*-band and my *hus*-band, they are friends." She glanced up at Gwen, meeting her eyes once more. "See?"

Gwen found herself shaking her head. "No, I don't understand, sorry."

"Hmm," the woman said, still staring at the backs of her hands laid flat on the dining table. "Your *hus*-band he likes the football, no?"

Gwen shrugged. "Yes, well, if you mean that he goes to the local team's football matches on Saturday, then yes, yes he does."

"Yes," the woman replied. "My *hus*-band and your *hus*-band they are friends from the football, do you see?"

"No, I can't say I do."

"Hmm, then maybe I can think of to put this like this." She glanced up, again for a fraction of a second, before returning to gaze at the backs of her hands. "The two of them, they do not like to watch the football here, so much, that is true?"

Gwen thought this over in her mind, studied it. That was true. The day that Floyd had suddenly come out with the idea that he was going to start going to the football had come as a great surprise to her, to say the least. And yet, she supposed, over the last three years it had just become pretty normal. She'd got to the point where she'd never given it so much as a second thought.

True, one day, when she'd been feeling particularly scorned, or something, she'd gone off and had a poke through his office. And, if Floyd was indeed using football for a pretence—as an *act* to cover for something else, then he was doing it extremely thoroughly.

Floyd had always been a hoarder, of just about everything. Those albums upon albums of faded and peeling old stamps were testament to that. Along with all those old-style, leather-bound, yellow-paged books he never seemed to read.

The ones that stank of mould and damp, and which came from those fleapit used bookstores he'd hunted them out from.

But when she'd gone through the office looking for clues of something—*any*thing—she had come across the football programmes, the little booklets from each match Floyd had been to. The little booklets that seemed extortionately priced at five pounds, at least from the ones that she'd quickly flipped through.

But the programmes had all been there.

The season tickets too, all stamped, torn, or whatever. All of that evidence that, whatever else Floyd might be doing, he was actually going to the ground and getting his ticket processed and picking up those programmes for each match.

Was it all just a sham?

Just an act?

She couldn't quite wrap her mind around it, although now, with the alcohol beginning to hum in her chest, and that half of a bottle still to go, she was readying herself to believe just about anything.

6

THE WOMAN had just left her last comment hanging over the table between them, not thinking to embellish it at all. And Gwen tried to think back over just how she'd put it, how the woman had put it, 'The two of them, they do not like to watch the football here, so much'.

When had Floyd *ever* seemed interested in football before that time three years ago? Never, as much as she could tell. He had never watched it on television, listened to it on the radio . . . he often cast off the sports pages of the newspaper and she'd use them for her seedlings, out in her greenhouse.

She looked over the table to the woman and said, "When did you arrive here, you know, to England?"

The woman steeped herself in silence once again, just staring at the backs of her hands, all of a sudden seemingly having become timid for the first time in their meeting.

Gwen wondered if she wanted more wine, but when she reached across the table to serve her more from the bottle, the woman shook her head and held her hand over her glass.

"No," she said, meeting Gwen's eye. "I need not more."

Gwen laid the bottle back down, with a slight glassy *tinkle* against the tablecloth.

The woman breathed a long and hard sigh, what Gwen could only think of as being a long-held and well-earned sigh. "We arrived here, to *Eng*-land, two months."

"Two months ago?"

"Yes," the woman said, with a wry smile, and a sharpness in her eyes. "Excuse please my English, because it is not perfect."

"That's quite all right."

"Yes, and we come to the city here, to live."

Gwen thought to ask why, but decided that now was the time

to keep her lips sealed, and to listen to what the woman had to say. She was, after all, for better or worse, about to either confirm or deny the suspicions she had surrounding Floyd.

And either way she *had* to know.

Another sigh, and then the woman continued, "Yes, and my *hus*-band, we come here from Hungary, and he likes the football, and so he say to me to go to the football, and so he go."

"I see."

"Yes, and when he go to the football he arrive home with the wine in his mouth, in his, how you say?"

"Breath."

"Yes," she said, "and with the goulash in his *breath*."

Gwen waited, trying her best to study the subtleties of this statement, to work out just what the insinuation was. But, no matter how hard she tried, she just couldn't. "And was that a problem?" Gwen said.

"Yes, because it is lie."

Gwen thought back to Floyd, how he'd been acting over the past two months. Had his behaviour been any different? She wasn't all that sure. He had been going off every other Saturday to watch the football for almost the last three years, so she supposed she'd just got so stuck into the routine so as not to analyse it any longer.

It just seemed mundane. Normal. But now, with it being thrust in her face, she *was* beginning to analyse it a little more.

The woman sighed again. "One day I . . . I . . ."

"Followed?"

"Yes, I follow him one day, and to the football stadium. And there, at the stadium, I see him with a man, another man."

Gwen knew just what was coming next.

"Your *hus*-band."

"I see."

"Yes," the woman said. "That was not a reason to be, uh, to be *sneaky*, but what occurred to me was to go with them, to *follow* them." She steepled her fingers and pressed them into her upper lip, and stared down at the tablecloth. "They go to a restaurant, they not go to football, and I watch them laugh and drink and I wait outside the restaurant and when they come out I follow them again."

Gwen felt her breathing shallow slightly, and her vision blurring a little around the edges, not at all sure what she should expect next.

"And," the woman continued, "I follow them on a bus, in taxi, and they come here, to here, to this *house*."

Gwen felt a prickling sensation in her chest, and her heart pounded a couple of times, and she was almost certain for a moment that she could feel the alcohol pumping round her circulatory system. "Here? To *this* house?"

"Yes," the woman said.

"And then what?"

The woman furrowed her brow, and stared more intently at the tablecloth, and then, in a very quiet voice, almost totally indistinct, she said, "Then they *kiss*."

7

I T WAS as if Gwen was falling.

Gwen caught a reminiscence of being a girl—a *little* girl again—and she thought back to being in a classroom. To the taste of rubbers at the end of pencils, to that smell of waxed wood that seemed to smother everything, to the ticking steel-framed clock that hung above the blackboard. And to that moment of weight-lessness as she leaned back in her chair, and somehow missed the wall behind her.

And she tumbled over with a *clatter* and *scrape*.

Then the sharp pain in her bottom, and her elbows, and the back of her head.

For a moment, in the present, Gwen felt herself leaning back in her chair, and the chair legs leaving the ground, and her falling down onto the slatted wooden floor with nothing to check her descent.

And then she realised that it was her mind that was moving, that her body was still, and that the whole world was swirling before her.

All at once she felt her stomach whine and pinch, and the chewed-up chicken nestled there seemed to compress and bite back at her. And she had to vomit. She just *had* to vomit.

But she remained where she was, apparently with her bottom fixed to the cushion of her chair, seemingly unable to move from her spot, staring out into space.

Before she really knew what was happening, she heard muffled sobs swabbing through the air, and, still stuck in her daze, she looked across the table, to the woman sat opposite her.

To Margit, as she recalled her name.

Maybe she should've felt solidarity, or maybe she should've felt a twin sense of anger. But all she could really feel in that moment was denial . . . no, less than that, not even denial—*numbness*.

The room continued to spin and she could hardly feel for the stem of her wine glass before her. But she did reach it, and she curled her fingers about it, and brought the glass up to her lips and she drank.

The alcohol ebbed through her.

When she parted her lips to speak all that came out was breath. She simply couldn't put anything into words.

"We wait for them," the woman said.

Gwen could only manage a curt nod as she attempted to get a grip on herself.

8

GWEN was well-attuned to the routines that existed between her and her husband. And, over the past few weeks, after she'd first felt that sense of something going on, that something which she could never get into the realm of identifying, she had grown even more detailed in her observations.

Somehow her body knew—it always knew—just when Floyd was going to arrive home. And, with that same instinctive magic, she always found herself tilting her head up to look at the large kitchen clock that ticked away, and seeing that it was around about six o'clock when he returned home.

Thinking about things now, about that day, it must've been about two months ago, when she'd looked up at the clock and seen it was only five thirty, and then Floyd had come in through the door. Half an hour early. That was what had triggered that stirring in her gut, made her think that something might be lurking beneath the surface, although she'd thought nothing consciously of it at the time.

The two of them, Gwen and the woman, both sat on the carpeted staircase, in the front hall of the house, both staring at the back of the front door intently.

Gwen was almost certain she could feel each second ticking by on the hand of her wristwatch, each tiny movement sending a shudder through her bones. An actual, perceptible shudder. And as each second passed she felt herself growing tighter and tighter wound up inside. So wound up that she was almost certain she would burst.

When her watch clicked over to twenty-five minutes past five, she got up, and, without a word, the woman got up too. Gwen shuffled up to the peephole in the front door and gazed out. No sign of them yet. But *soon*. They would be there soon.

All the possibilities reeled through her mind, that, perhaps, the woman's husband wouldn't come with Floyd that evening, or that *neither* of them would show up. Maybe they'd been plotting an elopement for weeks now, or ever since they'd met, and they'd already picked up on the subconscious signals that their wives had been sending.

Or perhaps—*just* perhaps—this was all a great big joke.

Some joke.

And then, distinctive, and impossible to miss, she heard the *scuff* of shoes against the pavement outside, and the low murmuring of voices.

Gwen could feel the woman's breathing on her cheek, that moist cloud of respiration, and she could hear her heartbeat, or what she thought was her heartbeat, also. The alcohol continued its twilight thrum through her system, giving off little jangles of hyperactivity wherever it lingered a moment or more.

She had no idea what she might do.

Would she screech, rush out the door and clobber the poor bastard to death?

. . . Or would she be more calculated, calm, wait without saying a word, pretending everything was fine, until Floyd had gone off to sleep, before sticking the kitchen knife between his ribs?

Only time would tell.

The footsteps got louder, and the voices more muffled.

Gwen pulled herself back from the peephole and took a long, deep, cleansing breath. She counted out the seconds, conscious of the ticking of her wristwatch's second hand. She could hear the woman's steady breathing too as she reached up to undo the latch on the front door.

9

THE TWO MEN, the woman's husband, and Gwen's husband, stood on the outside of the garden gate. Gwen's timing had been impeccable. The two men, still standing about a shoulder width apart, were touching their lips together in a way that reminded Gwen of a postcard she'd once seen of a pair of swans apparently 'kissing' at the beak.

Neither of the men moved, but both their sets of eyes rolled over Gwen, and the woman standing beside her. She could feel those slathering, scolded eyes lolling all over her.

What was she going to do?

Her heartbeat implored great, dignified action.

Her logical brain just told her to freeze.

In the end it was her gut that won out, the gut swimming with the half-digested chicken and well over three quarters of a bottle of white wine.

She turned to her side, and looked to the woman standing beside her, who wore a smouldering expression, and, with surety and neatness of action, surely brought on by the fading effects of the alcohol, she snatched her tight, made her sway, supported her in her arms, and pressed a hard, passionate kiss right on *her* lips.

As Gwen hung there, the woman in her arms, those tingles surging all over her flesh, she felt like some actor in a film, making some fair maiden swoon. And the thrill was almost too much for her pumping heart, for her knotted muscles, and when she looked up from the kiss, when she released the woman, she was met with a pair of extremely—*profoundly*—vacant glances.

And that made her glad.

ANOTHER NIGHT, ANOTHER OCCASION

1

J ACOB BUTTERLY thought that life was *pretty sweet* all things considered.

He looked himself over in the full-length mirror, the one with the gilded edged which, most likely, wasn't gold.

Fake tan on the cheeks—that'd been one of Mikey's brainwaves, *the genius!*—Winsor-knotted, tasteful navy-blue tie, that wouldn't upset the boat with his girlfriend's father, of that he was sure. A wide-shouldered jacket on top. A crisp, white shirt underneath. Cologne coming *out of his anus*. And a pair of freshly pressed trousers—straight from the dry cleaner's, even with that neat crease in the front of them and everything.

Yup, things were looking pretty sweet for the night ahead.

For this *meeting* with his girlfriend—Annie's—parents.

Oh, it wasn't a *swish* place or anything, or so she'd assured him several times over the phone . . . he'd already cottoned onto that thing that girls did, the way that if they said the same thing over and over again it really didn't matter if it was affirmative or negative, it was supposed to be taken as nothing less than full-bodied truth.

He flipped his minty gum over on his tongue, smudged it about his cheeks as if that might make his breath just a little fresher— fresher than he'd managed to get it after a good quarter of an hour brushing his teeth.

He felt great—really and truly great!

That throbbing, warm buzz inside of him.

Kind of squidging through his gut.

Making his blood feel thick.

And making his mind feel just a touch woozy.

Why, he couldn't think of a single thing that could go wrong with this dinner.

Meeting the parents—*no sweat!*

Why was it that people made such a big deal of it?

Why had there been so much as *films* made of it?

. . . Just a whole overblown detail, that was all it was.

And with that—slightly deep—thought thick in his mind's eye, he blew himself a kiss in the mirror and then headed on along the corridor, ready to catch the six-fifty bus which pulled out just at the end of the road.

2

THE RESTAURANT'S windows were perspiring.

That was the first thing that struck Jacob as he crossed the road—taking extra special care with the traffic, not wanting to get himself run down before he got the chance to show Annie's parents the *catch* he truly was—that'd make him look a right Wally!

The windows were perspiring from the inside. Clouds of steam from something or other—most likely a kitchen appliance of some sort?

Just beyond the perspiration, he could make out the flicker of candlelight, that familiar orangey glow.

It set his thoughts back to that time when, just after he'd arrived home from the office, briefcase in hand, and that weariness shredding his brain, to discover that Annie had already got into his house—he'd given her the spare key on their third date—and had lit a whole bunch of candles and had drawn herself a foamy bubble bath.

As he'd ditched his work shoes, hurriedly unknotted himself from his tie, and shucked his jacket, he hadn't even cared all that much that the candles were scented—that they had a rosemary *stink* to them that took him several trips to the dry cleaner to finally get out of his work clothes.

He didn't want the boys at work to start thinking he was a Nancy-boy, after all.

He inclined his neck. Took in the name of the restaurant.

Antonio's

Italian?

Greek?

Spanish?

. . . At the very least he was fairly certain that it would be *Mediterranean*.

Antonio, after all, was a very Mediterranean-sounding name.

He inspected himself briefly in the outward shine of the restaurant's windows, ripped off a stray thread from the lapel of his jacket, and then crossed on over the threshold of the place.

3

CONVERSATION BABBLED about the place. He caught that thick body heat straightaway. The heat that reminded him of the daily trawl to work on the Tube. Once he'd got over that familiar smell, he concentrated on the thick scent of rich dough carrying on the stifling air.

Pizza dough?

Was it something like that?

That made his mouth water.

Just thinking about the flavours.

The olives, the tomato paste, the lightly sautéed onions.

Delicious!

He glanced about the bobbing heads—every table apparently stuffed with either a couple or a family. All of them tucking into an earl*iesh* dinner.

He caught sight of Annie, and her parents, over in the corner of the place. All of them crammed in around a table with a white-and-red chequered cloth, and that Italian restaurant—he was *pretty* sure it was an Italian place now—standard of the candle stuffed into the green neck of a drained bottle of red wine.

They hadn't seen him.

Not yet.

Now was his chance.

Just a *moment* to catch his . . .

And then Annie spotted him.

Those walnut-coloured eyes of hers, alive with the flame of the candle before her, latched onto his.

He couldn't help but feel that reassuring warmth rising through him.

Not *unlike* that sensation he got before puking.

But *much* nicer.

After all, there most likely wasn't the sting of bile on the end of it . . .

He did his best to act *suave*, to *sashay* his way between the tables and towards Annie and her family. Actually, he thought that he did a pretty good job—which was to say that he didn't knock anyone, face first, into their dinner.

Annie's parents were sat with their backs to him. Only Annie watched him approach. But she hadn't alerted her parents that he had arrived, or at least so it seemed.

Only when Jacob took his place, at the head of the table, still standing, hands draped down by his sides—not wanting to push the boat out by stuffing one of his hands stylishly into a pocket in that way the *really cool* guys managed to pull off—did he finally get a look over the faces of her parents.

For some reason his heart stuck in his throat.

He supposed, for a second, he'd thought that there was *almost certainly* going to be something about this meeting which would throw him completely, and irretrievably, off his game. Like one—or *both*—of Annie's parents turning out to have been one of his teachers at school, or—*worse*—one of them turning out to be the PE teacher who'd walked in on him that time when he'd somehow shit himself while taking a leak at one of the urinals. And how that PE teacher—which for the life of him he couldn't remember the name of—had eyed him strangely as he'd waddled his way over to one of the cubicles with a *really* strange smile pressed on his lips . . .

But, gladly, they were completely unknown faces to Jacob.

Which was to say that he couldn't immediately place them anywhere familiar.

Good first step.

This *was* going to be a breeze.

Just like he'd hoped!

. . . How these things *always* turned out . . . it was only the incessant thinking which got the better of him—how his overactive imagination somehow got the better of him, tried to manipulate even the most innocuous of situations into somehow being a life-or-death showdown.

He extended his hand. Shook both parents' hands. Both had a firm shake on them. Both smiled back at him politely. They both just looked so *normal*. He couldn't quite get over it.

As he took up his place at the table, alongside Annie, he felt her take hold of his thigh, give it a firm squeeze. He was glad she chose to do so since he'd been deliberately trying to firm up his thighs in his sessions at the gym this week.

He took in Annie's parents properly for the first time.

Saw that her mother wore a prim, sensible dress with a cardigan drawn about her shoulders. He was glad to see that she'd aged pretty well. That her skin was more or less still shiny, and wrinkle-free, though the thought that she might've indulged in Botox did cross his mind . . . still, she had kept her figure—or if she'd once been fat at least it no longer showed . . . all good news if his designs on Annie were to be *long*-term.

Her father had those bustling, dark eyebrows. Tufts of grey hair sprouted from his scalp.

Like Jacob, he wore a jacket—a *black* jacket—along with a tie and shirt.

Jacob would've liked to have done a fist pump at picking the right tone and occasion with his dress, but he held himself back.

Because, after all, this evening was looking to turn out to be *one long success*.

Why, he was pretty sure that he'd make this The Best Evening of His Life.

Or, at the very least, he resolved to make it Top Ten.

And so, with jubilation rippling through just about every pore, he took Annie's father's invitation to pluck up his menu and have a paw through it for what he wanted to order.

"SAY WHAT?" Annie's father said, eyebrows furrowed, looking over his own menu at Jacob—eyeing him a little, well, what Jacob would've termed, *menacingly.*

Jacob smiled politely. Glanced up at the waiter: a moustached Italian—?—man with that thick, bristly black hair that always made him wonder if they dyed it like that, or if it was just a natural freak of genetics.

Jacob noticed how the waiter held tight onto his spiral-ringed notepad as if it might ease the obvious tension which had descended on the table right at this moment. The waiter's eyes bobbed between them all only stopping to land on Jacob's for that polite two-second interval before going back to scrutinising his notepad.

Finally, Jacob looked to Annie's father—to Steve, as he'd been told to call him. He felt a lump form in his throat but swallowed it back, then said, "Uh, spinach linguine."

"Ling what?" Steve said, still looking perplexed.

"Spinach linguine."

"And you like that, do you?"

Jacob slipped a sidelong glance first to Annie's mother—Margaret—and then to Annie herself, sitting beside him, though now not pressing her leg up against him as she had been doing till about thirty seconds ago.

For some reason, Jacob read a note of fear in Annie's eyes, and he instinctively knew that he'd done something wrong here.

But what?

The waiter finally thought to break in—to diffuse things. "I shall return with your drinks," he said.

And then, with a red-lipped smile full of pearly white teeth, he turned on his heel and dashed off, weaving his way between the red-and-white chequered tablecloths towards the kitchen.

And the steam which seemed to billow out of it.

Jacob breathed in deeply. Felt the stifling air fill his lungs, cause his shoulders to rise up—to *arch* back. Perfect moment to change the subject now. Best to take advantage of it as soon as possible.

And so, with the latest rugby headline fresh on his tongue—Annie had briefed him beforehand that her father, that *Steve*, loved rugby—he did his best to meet Steve's steely gaze.

But, before he so much as made a *peep*, Steve spoke.

"I mean, what's that got in it"—and he wrinkled up his nose as if he was smelling something deeply unpleasant—"*spinach linguine?*"

A little disappointed that he wouldn't get the opportunity to use his, Wikipedia-acquired, knowledge to have a quick chinwag about Adrian Nappleswick, and his apparently *fascinating*—not to mention *prolific*—try-scoring abilities, Jacob turned his mind back to the subject at hand.

This apparently perennial-subject.

"Well," Jacob said, slipping Annie a glance once more, and wishing that they'd made the drinks order *before* they'd ordered their food . . . and not done both at the same time, "it's a kind of pasta, and it's got a sort of pesto sauce—I think—and it's flavoured with spinach."

"No meat, then?"

Jacob looked to Annie's mother—*Margaret*—and he was pretty sure that he saw that same note of warning in *her* eyes, that same note of warning he'd just seen from Annie herself.

Like mother, like daughter.

Yes, it was a little like that.

Jacob looked back across the table to Steve, saw how he was gripping tight to the tablecloth, almost as if they'd suddenly been transported onto a cruise-liner and they'd found themselves stuck in a particularly rotten storm . . . well, actually, that wasn't *at all* how it would be like considering that Annie had told him that Steve had once served in the Navy . . . so Jacob was fairly certain that a bit of rough water wouldn't be too much for a salt-skinned seadog, like Steve apparently was, to handle.

Jacob shook his head. "No, there's no meat in it."

Steve threw up his hands. His eyes blazed wide. His nostrils seemed to take on individual—and extremely *furious*—personalities of their own.

The way that he wheeled about, the way that he threw up his hands and stared at his wife and daughter made it seem like Steve had just come across what was—surely—the greatest injustice of his natural existence.

To say Jacob felt just a little *squeaky-bum-time* was putting it lightly.

Once Steve had composed himself—or *not* as the case might've been—he shifted his gaze, his *fury*, back onto Jacob. "Don't tell me," he said, then took a quick breath as if this was something that needed to be said with extreme caution—an accusation that really couldn't be made without all the ducks in a row, without all the evidence lined up and ready to be dispensed in rapid-fire fashion. "Don't tell me you're a *vegetarian*."

Jacob was extremely glad that the waiter chose that exact moment to arrive back at the table. To offer the bottle of wine to Steve so that he might taste it. Slosh it about in his glass a while. Sniff at it. And then, of course, they endured that stilted silence while the waiter poured them all their first glass.

After all that hassle, Jacob was kind of hoping that the previous conversation would be forgotten.

But that turned out to be just a *touch* naïve.

Over the rim of his glass, Steve eyed Jacob. "So, then, what is it?"

Jacob bit hard into his lower lip. Glanced to Annie, then to her mother, and then back to Steve once again.

How else was he supposed to respond?

So he just settled on a nod.

5

I F JACOB had been told ahead of time to avoid certain things with Annie's father—if Annie had clued him in, *just a little*—then he would've felt like he'd done something wrong.

That he was *accountable* in some way.

However, the way things had fallen, the way this evening had happened to turn out, he really felt a sense of injustice above all else.

Well, it was like Annie's father was blaming him for just being himself—for him being *vegetarian*.

And, anyway, what was the issue with it?

Why was it such a big problem?

It wasn't like Jacob had any designs on marrying Steve himself or—God forbid—living together with him.

No, it was more of a case that Steve would need to tolerate Jacob for the odd visit, now and again, the odd Christmas Day, Easter . . . that sort of thing . . .

They sat in stiff silence till the food arrived, though Margaret made a few ill-fated attempts to strike up conversation.

She asked Jacob a few things, of course, but Jacob couldn't really bring himself to elaborate on his one-line answers with Steve glaring at him from Margaret's side.

Jacob was so indescribably glad when the food arrived that he almost forgot his manners completely. Almost just dug right into his delicious, gently steaming spinach linguine.

And he might well have done so if it hadn't been for the way he'd caught Steve staring at his plate, the way that he seemed to be *eyeballing* it like it had just gone and driven over his mother, or something.

What had spinach linguine ever done to Steve?

The waiter poured them out more wine. Served some sparkling

water too for those who wanted it. Then he passed a nervous, flickering glance between them—that glance from a waiter which Jacob always imagined represented the thought: *I'm so glad I'm not sitting at* that *table.*

Jacob picked up his cutlery, doing his best to keep up the increasingly false smile on his lips. When he looked about the table, to the others' orders, he noted the bolognaises: thick red sauce, sloppy spaghetti, and, of course, lashings of meatballs.

They'd, all of them—all *three* of them—ordered the same thing.

Jacob found himself clutching his knife and fork a little tighter than he would've liked, and could already feel the sweat leaking on out of his forehead, beading its way down the sides of his face.

This place *was* just a little hot.

Lots of people all stuffed into a fairly tight restaurant.

Jacob worked to cut up his pasta while he felt the unmistakable weight of Steve's glare heavy on him. It made him twitch just a little. Sent him back to those times when he'd been at school and the teacher had apparently been staring at him, waiting for him to answer some question they'd dished out.

It was no way to eat.

And this situation was just growing *increasingly* ridiculous.

Why, there might not be a better time to clear the air, to nip to the quick of this whole fallout.

So, despite his grumbling tummy, and feeling the warmth from the wine flooding up to his cheeks—the dry flavour of the wine bathing his mouth—he squared his shoulders and stared right back at Steve.

"What's the problem?" Jacob said.

Steve looked a little blank a couple of moments. Then he set his own cutlery down by the side of his plate.

Jacob was very aware of both the ladies—Margaret and Annie—looking on at them with frightened expressions.

He didn't even have to look them over to know that.

"Look," Jacob said, determined to get this over with reasonably and *efficiently*, "I get that you don't like vegetarians, whatever reason that might be, and that I should've gone ahead and ordered the spaghetti bolognaise. Sorry. I'm *very* sorry I didn't, believe me."

Jacob could feel his pores all flushing out sweat at a rate of knots now, and he would've liked to have removed his jacket if he hadn't feared interrupting his flow.

He turned his attention back to his plate, eyeing it as innocuously as he possibly could, or, maybe, trying to make out that it was as *innocuous* as could be.

"Go on, then," Jacob said. "What's the problem, eh?"

At that moment Jacob speculated later that he might've liked to feel Annie's reassuring touch at his thigh, beneath the level of the table.

But there was no *touch* to be had.

Maybe he should've taken it as a sign.

But he wasn't in the habit of taking *anything* as a sign.

Steve seemed to fill up like a hot-air balloon—the way that they get when they're being prepared for take-off, which is to say that he began all pretty much spread out across the ground, deflated, and then, slowly and surely, filled up with hot air till reaching the point of bursting . . . or the point of take-off, depending on how far Jacob wished to stretch the metaphor.

In any case, Jacob could say for sure that it looked very likely that, with all the hot air filling Steve, he might well lift right on up off his seat, rise to the ceiling and bump against it a few times before someone saw fit to pop him with a pin . . .

Steve stayed put, though.

Just about.

Though Jacob had to pinch himself to be sure he wasn't delusional.

"*Outside*," Steve said.

Jacob felt that fresh, rather warm, wave of confidence ride back a little. He guessed that might be the rush of alcohol retreating—his cold-eyed sobriety making an appearance.

In any case, he saw reason enough to respond, "Uh, what?"

Steve, Jacob now saw, had gritted his teeth.

And beyond Steve, Jacob made out the several dozen faces of the other diners, now watching on, all of them forming a raggedy patchwork—a *backdrop*—to this little foray.

And Jacob guessed that, maybe, one or both of them had spoken a little loudly.

"I said," Steve repeated, and then carefully enunciated, "*Out. Side.*"

6

COMPARED with the stifling heat of the restaurant, the air in the road outside was cool and somewhat—even given the circumstances—*refreshing*.

Jacob noticed how several people had followed them outside: all mostly middle-aged men, about Steve's age, all of them swigging from their glasses of red wine, some chattering among themselves.

At the steamed-up window of the restaurant, Jacob made up the unsmiling and—he was glad to see—*extremely concerned* female faces: wives and mothers and sisters and daughters and aunties and cousins, and . . .

Jacob brought Steve into focus before him.

Watched on as he shrugged his jacket off his shoulders, another of the onlookers—one of the middle-aged men—taking it from him and folding it neatly over his arm.

When Jacob glanced to the doorway of the restaurant, he noted their waiter standing there, leading against the doorframe, an unlit cigarette dangling from his lips, droopy bags hanging from his eyes and giving the distinct impression that this sort of thing happened just about every day of the week . . . or, at the very least, on Saturday nights like this one.

Jacob watched as Steve turned back to face him, as he rolled up the sleeves of his pristine, white shirt, shrugged his shoulders, apparently getting them loosened up.

All of a sudden Jacob felt very small, standing here, in this street, in his own suit, with all these middle-aged men who had previously been anonymous strangers—eating in the restaurant with them—boxing him in . . .

Jacob glanced about himself, naïvely half hoping that there might be the blue flash of police lights to be had.

There wasn't.

"Come on, then," Steve said, voice gruff and yet strangely even, and a little *more* worryingly—*sober*.

Jacob glanced about himself, wondering if he might get a hint off someone.

But, nope, just mean, *middle-aged* male faces.

Looking grim and unsympathetic.

Worse, actually . . . looking *enthusiastic*.

He noticed a pair of men—both of them smartly dressed in their own suits—exchange a wad of notes between them.

Worse, he noticed that they seemed to be five-pound notes.

Was this what the evening had been reduced to: low-stakes gambling?

He looked back to the restaurant window, hoping to catch sight of Annie there . . . but he couldn't see her. He wondered if she'd maybe been so overwhelmed by all this that she'd gone to cry her eyes out in the toilets with only her mother for solace.

He could only hope.

Steve had his sleeves rolled back to the elbow now, and he held his fists up to his chest—clenched in that way that boxers do. His cheeks were aflame with a pinkish glow, from the wine, or from fury, Jacob wasn't one-hundred-percent sure which.

Jacob blinked a few times. Tried to work out if he might've found himself struck down by a daze. If he might have been imagining all this. Like he'd hit his head, or something.

Or something.

. . . But, nope, this was all really happening.

Steve took a couple of steps towards him. Fists still raised. He was about five, six paces away now, and Jacob got the feeling that —from where he stood—he could most likely catch Jacob pretty smartly with one—if not both—of his knuckles.

"Put 'em up, son," Steve said.

Jacob held his arms down by his sides, not wanting to entice the maniac any further, though it did appear that hopes for a democratic resolution were swiftly fading . . . and now that there was money on the line—albeit not *his* money—it felt strangely more real.

As Steve bounced from one foot to the other, looking surprisingly nimble for the podge about his stomach, he said, "Used to do this to snot-nosed kids in the Navy—teach them a lesson."

Jacob just stood there, still stunned, till he felt sure hands behind him. One of the middle-aged men spectating, forcing his arms up from his sides, up to his chest.

So that Jacob assumed the defensive position.

The position that might well get him killed.

"That's it, boy," Steve said, a wide smile forming on his lips.

Jacob closed his eyes. Felt his insides kind of crunch in on themselves. His heart skipped a half dozen beats. Then he squeezed his fingers tighter—making fists.

He waited for the pummelling to come.

Waited for the first feel of knuckle against cheekbone.

The first earth-shattering *craaack!*

But it didn't come.

He breathed in that cheesy smell of the restaurant.

Felt his mouth salivate strangely.

Like he was just about to take a mouthful.

Maybe . . . maybe *none* of this was happening, perhaps this was just some sort of a crazy mirage, and he was still sat there, at the table, with his would-be father-in-law, alongside his would-be —*might-be*—future wife . . . and when he opened his eyes he truly believed, believed that he'd grown so tense, become so overwrought by the whole encounter, that he had thrown himself into this . . . this *nightmarish* fantasy.

He opened his eyes.

But it was still the same.

Out here, in the street.

Steve circling.

Lips peeling back.

The fist drawing over his shoulder.

The flash of flesh in the orangey glow of the streetlights.

Jacob's instincts worked faster than his brain.

He ducked.

Listened to that fresh *swoosh!* of fist displacing air above his head.

He crouched down, was sure he would tumble over, fall flat on his face.

But he kept himself stable.

Noticed his fists still clenched.

And then . . . and then . . . the *craziest* thought struck him . . . no, that was *wrong* . . . because, in reality, what happened was that Jacob's fist struck *Steve* . . . on the back of his head . . . sent *him* tumbling over . . . barrelling down . . . landing *hard* onto the curb . . . making a spine-tingling *crunch!* as he landed.

7

F OR THE FIRST FEW SECONDS, Jacob felt nothing at all—nothing save for the numbness.

The *nothingness*.

And then his blood began to buzz.

His brain thickened, swelled.

His heart leaped out of its inactivity—plucked on again with its, standard, unchecked steadiness.

And then his surroundings came back. The grunts and grumbles of the men about him. He watched one of the men palm the wad of notes back to the other, and then that same man, the one who'd ended up with the notes, make his way back towards the doorway of the restaurant, giving Jacob a well-done clap on the shoulder as he went . . . yes, now—*now*—they were all leaving, breaking up this impromptu fight, heading back to their dinners, the entertainment now done with . . . the waiter had disappeared from the doorway, headed back inside following his non-smoking break . . .

Still feeling that rippling numbness pass through him, Jacob turned his attention back to Steve, lying on his front, prostrate on the ground, apparently unconscious.

Jacob looked about him, to the rapidly diminishing crowd. "Uh," he started, somewhat unconvincingly, "anyone here a doctor?"

He was only greeted by silence, and those same men continued to head on back through the doorway, back to their waiting dinners . . . he guessed that some of them had no doubt begun to have their dessert, or coffees . . . he wondered dizzily if those hypothetical coffees would still be warm by the time they got back . . . for their sakes he hoped so . . .

Soon enough, Jacob was left alone, just him and the apparently unconscious Steve.

It was then that he noticed Margaret and Annie emerge from the doorway of the restaurant. He didn't need to linger or ponder extensively to see those looks of disgust spread out over their faces to know that he certainly wasn't going to end up on the sympathetic side of tonight.

And so, with a muttered apology, nothing more than an under-the-breath mumble, he made steady progress away from the restaurant, away from Annie and her fallen father, and towards that rather-nice-looking curry takeaway on the corner.

It'd probably be better to speak about this later.

Tomorrow, maybe, when the dust had settled . . .

OPERATION

THE SMELL OF THE DISINFECTANT on the hospital emergency room floor really got up Harriet's nose. Sometimes—in her more egomaniacal turns—she wondered if the world was out to specifically annoy her.

She could still taste the gravy from the turkey sandwich she had been eating about an hour ago. About an hour before her father had managed to take a tumble down the stairs.

Just as was family tradition—or so her father assured her—they'd only got through about an eighth of the turkey during Christmas Day, and so had had to store the rest in the fridge. And, of course, this meant all sorts of uses, from, but not restricted to: turkey soup, turkey on toast, and even turkey curry. But after they'd dipped their toes in that amount of invention, they'd settled back into the old standard:

The turkey sandwich.

Harriet pressed her back into the blue plastic chair of the emergency room. There was a scrap of a cushion beneath her backside, but it did nothing to ward away any of the numbness, and she could already feel pins and needles digging into her thighs and lower back. She would probably wake up tomorrow all stiff and unruly.

Looking about the emergency room, Harriet had to admit that it was—among the half a dozen or so she had visited in the course of her life—somewhat *boxy*.

And, also, strangely deserted.

She supposed that was the difference between living in the city, and living out in the countryside, as her father did.

Over to her left, she spotted a child dressed in a light-green football kit. One of his white socks was still pulled up to the knee, while the other was rolled all the way down to the ankle, and, at about his shin, there was a taped-on bandage through which the blood already seeped.

It left a rusty brown trace on the otherwise white bandage.

That wasn't what Harriet found annoying, though, what she found annoying was the way that the boy was constantly *tap-tapping* the studs of his football boots against the blue laminate flooring of the emergency room.

Tap.

Tap.

Tap-tap. Tap.

Tap-tap-tap-tap.

Tap.

Harriet looked over the boy's mother, and saw that she was in a virtual world, her fingers skittering over the screen of her mobile phone, inattentive to her offspring.

The boy was just glancing about the emergency room.

Bored.

When Harriet looked up again, she realised that there was a white-coated doctor standing there. He wore thin-framed, steel-grey glasses, and held a clipboard. His complexion was pale, but maybe it was the effect of his contrasting black hair. He pushed his glasses back up his straight, bony nose, and read out Harriet's full name.

Surname, and all.

Harriet felt a slight stirring in her gut at the fact that the doctor had used her birth surname. Her *father's* surname. But she knew that her anger was misplaced. It wasn't the doctor's fault, after all. It was her father who had been so impertinent as to give her identity the way he had.

Harriet shifted off her seat and followed the doctor down another disinfectant-stinking corridor. She was glad to find that the *tap-tap* of the football studs had been replaced by the gentle *hum* of either lighting, or machines, or whatever else it might be.

As they turned the corner of the corridor, the doctor stifled a yawn with the back of his hand, and, for the first time, Harriet noted the deeply engrained dark circles beneath the doctor's eyes. She supposed that the holiday shifts were somewhat brutal.

Perhaps he was a more junior member of the staff, and so had been thrown the whole truckload of cases while the senior doctors went off skiing, or to some Caribbean island, or to some other exotic *doctors'* holiday destination.

The doctor led Harriet in through a doorway, to a smallish examination room.

Harriet's father—or *Doug*, as she always insisted on calling him out loud—was stretched out on the flimsy table, the green, paper sheet beneath him a little crinkled under his weight.

Her dad's face was still wrinkled with pain, and Harriet made out her father's exposed, paper-skinned arm. There was the deep purple bruise, and the large swelling. When her father had taken his tumble, he had insisted that they not make a fuss about it. That his arm would get better on its own. Harriet had thought long and hard about letting her 'old man' get his wish, she was leaving tomorrow, but, in the end, she had decided against it.

After all, her father was now *that age* when the carer and *caree* roles had been well and truly reversed . . . and even if her father hadn't held his end of that particular bargain, Harriet knew that she would find it gut-wrenchingly difficult not to do the Right Thing.

This—*all this*—had just been a sort of fluke, a strange twisting of the fates, and though she wasn't anywhere close to being spiritually inclined, far from it what with her having a decent teaching position as a physics lecturer at a university, she had to admit that there was some sort of 'unseen' at play within this interaction.

Harriet had broken up with her husband less than a month earlier.

Her father's girlfriend—was that how Harriet should refer to her, or was 'partner' the more apt?—had succumbed to a long battle with cancer only a week or so afterwards.

It had seemed like the thing to do.

Harriet had no family, and all her pseudo family—the friends she had accrued throughout her life—had gone forth and multiplied. They had gone fully nuclear.

No tacked-on, honouree aunts required.

She had thought, somewhat fatalistically, that she would be killing two birds with one stone by coming to see her father for Christmas.

That she would quench their loneliness at the loneliest time of the year.

But that wasn't *quite* how it had turned out.

She approached her father, lying on the examination table.

His eyes sought out hers, and she observed the frown lines— apparently expressing pain—retreat back into his skin as he saw her there.

"Harry," he said, his voice raspy, and his whole body making an effort to get out so much as *that* sound.

He tried out a vague smile on her.

Harriet found herself smiling back.

The doctor, Harriet could feel, had something to say.

Doctors *always* had something to say.

"Ms Lunder," the doctor said, making certain to buzz the 'Ms' hard as he again used her father's surname, "I was just telling your father that we're going to need to operate. That we need to put some pins into his arm, to help the bone to mend."

Harriet looked to her father, saw that there was a slight concern sketched across his face.

Oh, God, didn't he like needles?

Had his attempt to avoid the hospital been some kind of surface response to some deep-seated fear of all things medical?

The doctor went on.

"We're going to take him into theatre right away—everything's ready to go."

Harriet looked to her father, to his mahogany-shaded eyes.

Could she see some tears glistening there?

"Okay," Harriet replied, not really feeling like she was adding much to the conversation.

The doctor turned his attention to Harriet's father. "Mr Lunder, how's the pain? Are you sure you wouldn't like us to give you something?"

Harriet's father shook his head, and managed a raspy, "No."

The doctor seemed to hold in a sigh. The way his eyes traced his sockets seemed to imply that he was considering rolling his eyes the moment he left the room. "Okay, then," the doctor said. "A porter will be by soon, all right?"

The doctor slipped from the room, adjusting his glasses as he went, and dangling his clipboard down by his side.

Off to go and see another emergency case, Harriet supposed.

Perhaps to see to the boy and his football injury.

Harriet looked back to her father, unable to really think of anything to say.

She thought about their Christmas so far, and how—*between themselves*—they had managed to vanquish any uncomfortable silence by either flipping on the TV, or by clicking on the radio. When all else failed, Harriet would ask if they needed anything from the shop, and she would trundle on out, in her second-hand hatchback, to the shop just down the road.

Once or twice, when she did slip out to get something or other, she found the tears—*inexplicably*—rolling down her cheeks. She had had to pull over, onto the curb. And, before she knew it, she'd be bashing away at the steering wheel, feeling the force of her blows rock through the car, flustering the suspension.

By the time she got back to the house, though, her stoic exterior would be very much back intact, and she would turn her mind to whatever it was that needed seeing to.

Her father, she soon surmised following her arrival to his neat, cute—if not a little small—bungalow, had been living in comparable filth. Harriet hadn't been quite able to stitch together just whether this was part of the grieving process, or for the simple fact that his deceased *partner* had been the one on cleaning duty.

Or maybe they'd both lived there all along.

Harriet recalled setting foot in the place and, almost immediately, feeling overpowered by the stench of sour milk and rotten eggs. After her father had offered her the welcome cup of tea in a cup which, by the look of the sallow stains up its sides, didn't seem to have been washed in months, Harriet excused herself in the politest manner possible and swept out to aforementioned shop to buy up almost their entire stock of cleaning utensils and bleach.

After a good day's work, Harriet had, more or less, got the whole place clean.

The doctor having left, and the two of them now having to await the arrival of the orderly in the examination room, Harriet looked back to her father's injury. To that welt on his arm, and how the blackened bruise seemed to seep out from the afflicted area like some nightmarish spider web.

"Harry?" her father said.

Harriet did her best not to wince at this. She had battled for most of her life for acquaintances—and she still regarded her father in that category—to stop unsexing her with that particular nickname. But she hadn't thought to correct her father.

It hadn't seemed right to.

"Hmm," Harriet said, still standing a good few paces from where her father lay.

Then, when Harriet glanced down, she saw that he was extending his hand—the hand of his good arm—in her direction. And that he wanted to take her hand in his own.

Her mind flexed about within the confines of her skull. She thought about how, in the course of the previous week, they had hardly had much physical contact beyond the awkward, single, dry peck on the cheek when she had arrived.

Whichever milieu they had stumbled across: kitchen, sitting room, dining room; they had both, by some kind of an unspoken oath, chosen to sit just as far apart as they could manage.

And Harriet could recall how, each time, she would sit with her hands clasped and subconsciously lean herself away from her father.

Because, no matter what she told herself—no matter what she told herself about what she *felt*—she knew that this was weird.

No way around it.

It *was* weird.

Harriet had had her father's details for such a long time. She had contacted him, maybe, ten years ago. Found out that her mother had been long dead. And yet she hadn't thought to actually reach out to her father, to have a *physical* meeting with him until the moment she had broken up with her husband a month before.

Why she had thought to dig out that slip of paper she'd thought had been long-forgotten, at the bottom of that drawer which contained her undergraduate thesis and other useless scraps of paper.

Harriet felt the colours in the examination room sharpen. The fluorescent strip-bulb above her head seemed to be pulsating gently, but the motion was enough to make her nauseous. She really would have liked to get out of the hospital. To go someplace else.

Back home.

But she had no home any longer.

She had told her husband that he could remain there.

Harriet pushed her father's outstretched hand to the very periphery of her vision, and she turned her attention back to her father's injury. She breathed in deep, feeling that unpleasant, dry chemical taste start up again at the back of her throat. "Why didn't you accept the painkillers?" Harriet said.

Her father remained silent.

She could hear his slightly snatched breaths.

And she could tell he was in pain.

When Harriet turned to look at him, she saw that he was now looking into mid-air. Although he continued to hold out his hand to her, there was no real effort put into the gesture. His hand was limp now. A sort of forgotten offering.

"Is it . . .?" Harriet began, and felt her voice fail her.

She had always found it near impossible to speak with an open heart—to articulate her emotions—and she was having difficulty letting go right now.

But she forced herself along.

The sooner she got it out of her, the sooner it would all be over.

"Are you, you know," Harriet tried again, "Punishing yourself?"

Her father didn't reply. He continued to stare into mid-air.

Apparently deeply focussed on something within his own mind.

Perhaps he was thinking about his dead partner—the woman Harriet had never known.

Or maybe he was thinking about something altogether different.

Harriet really had no grasp at all on her father.

The two of them were so different what with her being a physicist, and him being a retired contractor . . . it was almost as if they didn't share the same country, let alone the same language.

"Dad?" Harriet said, the word feeling alien in her throat.

The first time she hadn't directly addressed him as 'Doug'.

Her father gave a pair of blinks. It seemed to clear his vision. He turned his attention back onto her. He blinked again. A slight smile formed on his lips. He reached out his hand once more, and, this time, feeling a new force passing through her, Harriet took it.

"It's okay, Dad," Harriet said, "Everything's going to be fine."

And, with a gentle *squeak* of unoiled wheels, the porter turned the corner and entered the examination room, ready to take Harriet's father away for his operation.

Harriet would wait for him.

She would play the daughter.

For now.

DON'T TELL ME I'M
NOT OKAY

1

THE WORST PART about Mechanics 101—the class which Tara had been compelled to take to get herself 'caught up' on the more practical areas of mathematics—was the lecture hall.

With its hard, mottled wooden panelling all over the place.

That rotten smell of pine—was it pine?—the way it left her with a dry taste in her mouth. How, whenever her fingertips mistakenly came into contact with the underside of the table, to smooth down her skirt, or to get something from her bag, she would be forced to touch the several hundred—she was sure—pieces of dried-up gum stuck there.

Then there was the draught.

God, what she would've given to have a modicum of warmth in the room.

The draught blew in underneath the door to the lecture hall sounding for all the world like a wind howling through a desert valley.

Even in her metaphors, she craved heat.

But *was* the room the very worst of it?

Perhaps it was the lecturer.

Mr Smith.

That strange, everyman, anybody name.

And the way that he wore his tweed suits—with the leather elbow patches—without any observable sense of irony. And how he constantly kept his hands locked together at the base of his spine, and walked back and forth at the front of the lecture theatre, staring a little upwards into space in the way that only *academics* could do.

His voice, well, Tara was sure that he could *quite easily* sell himself to some sort of a sleep therapy company . . . she was sure that he would be far more successful doing that than being a lecturer, or, at least, a lecturer that anybody would actually listen to.

What Tara wouldn't give for a window in this place, just some scrap of hope that she might be able to escape. Some sign of the outside world. It seemed like the whole lecture hall was designed to smother out any recollection the student might have of any world beyond the green chalkboard with its yellow chalk scribbled all over it in illegible loops and lines.

She did want to get out.

Get *out* of here.

But she knew that she had to get through the module.

If she failed to do so, she wouldn't be able to follow her true passion.

Follow her interests in imaginary numbers.

She would fall at the first hurdle.

As Mr Smith's tones continued to drawl about the lecture hall, Tara could feel something in her eye. At first she attempted to ignore it, to blink it away. But she couldn't. Whatever it was: a small piece of gravel, lint . . . a *fly?* . . . she couldn't manage to get shot of it.

Nothing else she could do except reach up and, with the very tip of her fingernail, attempt to dislodge the object, whatever it was.

She went at the object for a solid minute and a half—she knew because she counted out the seconds, a habit of hers with Mr Smith's lectures—but no dice.

She withdrew her fingernail, giving the attempt up as lost, coming to terms with the fact that she would have to take a proper look once she had got through with this lecture . . . if it ever *did* end.

"You okay?"

The whispered voice came from Tara's left-hand side.

She glanced in its direction, and, at the same time, felt a slight shudder run up her spine. Though Mr Smith was just about the most docile of lecturers to be had, he did make a point of calling out to anybody who decided to chat while he rambled on. And if there was anything which Tara *really* couldn't stand, it was being the centre of attention.

Especially for a dressing down.

She tried—and failed—to swallow the dry taste out of her mouth, and breathed in yet more of the rotten pine smell of the lecture hall. Then she eyed the whisperer.

A boy . . . the whole *hall* was filled with boys. Though there were a fair amount of girls on her maths course, they had all, apparently, whistled through mechanics just fine. Which left Tara alone here, to face this whole hall of *boys.*

The boy in question, she quickly identified as Paul.

Paul was on the large side and he wore baggy jeans and baggy hooded tops in an apparent attempt to hide the fact. He always wore a baseball cap too, squeezed down over his black, greasy and —as Tara had unfortunately noticed—*dandruff-ridden* hair.

Tara managed the vaguest of vague smiles and then turned her attention back to the front of the hall, back to Mr Smith as he babbled on. "I'm fine," she said, out of the corner of her mouth, so quiet that it hardly qualified as so much as a whisper.

And that should've been the end of it, or, at least, Tara had expected as much.

However, as it turned out, it *wasn't* the end.

"You're crying," Paul said, his voice slightly louder this time.

Tara didn't turn to look at him. She kept facing forwards. She glanced down at her pad of notes where she had scribbled just whatever Mr Smith had written up on the board during the lecture. She admitted to herself that this material was just about as opaque as it had been right from the start. Mechanics, she decided, really made no sense whatsoever to her.

"Hey?"

This time there came a whisper from the right-hand side.

Tara couldn't help but look, acting on nothing but instinct.

She caught sight of Thom.

He was blond, slim and wore nothing but t-shirts and cargo shorts—and *sandals*—all year around.

"Are you okay?" Thom asked.

Tara looked to him, smiled slightly, then nodded.

When she turned back to the front, she saw that Mr Smith had stopped in his pacing and that he was staring right at her. She felt her heart stick in her throat for several seconds. Her blood ran hot, and then cold. She found herself staring back into Mr Smith's eyes. He held her gaze for seconds that felt like years and then—mercy of all mercies—he continued his stroll, and his lecture.

Tara gripped her pen tighter and jotted down a nonsense formula in the margin of her page hoping that the two boys—one on either side, *surrounded now!*—would forget this whole thing. What *was* it about a woman crying that instantly brought a whole bunch of male attention? . . . And, anyway, it wasn't like she was even crying in the first place! She just had something stuck in her eye.

The next minute or so was blissfully quiet.

Ominously quiet.

When Tara glanced up she saw that both Thom and Paul were staring at her.

Tara laid her pen down a touch too hard on her desktop—well, maybe she *slammed* it down actually. She had hoped that this gesture would break the boys' concentration, but, instead, it brought the whole of the lecture hall's attention right onto her.

Tara felt the flush rising in her cheeks, and her blood chilling to well below freezing.

She could barely bring herself to glance up, and to see Mr Smith standing there, at the front of the lecture hall, with a bemused look on his face.

"Is everything quite all right up there?" he said.

Tara felt like the blood might break through the surface of her skin at any second. But she sank her teeth into her bottom lip and managed a nod.

Mr Smith, not to mention the rest of the hall, continued to stare at her for a good few seconds before, with a hard sigh, Mr Smith resumed his pacing back and forth . . . back and forth . . . back and forth until, finally—*mercifully*—the bell sounded for the end of the hour.

2

TARA DID HER BEST to escape Paul and Thom, but she found them on her tracks pretty much as soon as she'd set foot outside of the lecture hall. She tried to keep her focus fixed on the double doors ahead, and the glimmering, golden sunlight beyond. From how she'd been feeling in the hall—which was to say *cold*—she'd imagined that she'd surface from the lecture hall to a snow-covered landscape.

She wasn't really sure which she would've preferred.

The corridor outside the lecture hall had a whole bunch of photographic portraits hanging down off the wall. All the past vice-chancellors of the university. All of them with those gnarled, half-smiles fixed on their lips. In a whole variety of poses, but mostly with their hands clutched beneath their chins.

Outside the lecture hall at least it didn't stink of rotten pine, and the dry taste was shifting from Tara's mouth. At least she had *something* to thank the fates for.

She could still hear the percussive pursuit of both Paul and Thom, though, the two of them not giving up yet.

"Are you sure you're okay?" Paul said. "I mean, if something's the matter, you can talk to us, we're good listeners."

"Yeah," Thom put in, "we're *great* listeners."

Tara reached the double doors at the end of the corridor and she shoved them open. The sunlight rushed over her, warming her cheeks and her blood. The verdant lawns of the university stretched out before her and she couldn't help but feel a little positive about the blue skies which soared above.

Birds were chirruping too, but Tara had always been fairly indifferent about birds.

"Where're you going?" Paul said.

"Home," Tara replied, trying her best to make her tone as snappy as possible.

"Aren't you going to tell us what's wrong?" Thom said.

Annoyingly—*really* annoyingly—she could still feel the bit of grit, or whatever it was, still stuck in her eye, *forcing* her to keep crying out of her single eye.

She looked back over them and decided that now it was time to bring out the Big Guns. "Women problems," she said.

Thom and Paul stopped following her then, they lagged back, and Tara headed on, towards the bus stop, ready to get away from the campus for a while. She would feel much better about this whole thing—slightly less mortified about having been called attention to in the middle of the lecture hall—when she got back home in her boxy little room, got herself surrounded by her books.

But when she glanced back over her shoulder, she saw that both Thom and Paul were *still* following her . . . albeit somewhat sheepishly.

What would it take to shake them off for good?

"Look," she said, turning to face the two of them straight on, "what'll it take for you two to leave me alone?"

Thom and Paul exchanged glances.

She was certain that the two of them had slipped several shades of pale in the past few minutes . . . ever since she'd mentioned the Women Problems.

"A drink?" Thom finally got out.

"Huh?" Tara said.

Thom exchanged glances with Paul, and Paul nodded back. "We'd like to take you out for a drink."

Tara tried to get this through her brain, tried to understand just what the hell this was about. But she found herself speaking before she'd really got the whole thing a hundred-percent clear. "Both of you?"

Another exchange of glances between Paul and Thom, and then

Thom said, "Yeah." Paul nudged Thom in the ribs, and then Thom added, "To talk about your problems."

Tara breathed in deep and long, tried to bring herself from saying something mean, or hard-hearted. But what was she supposed to say to these two? For a start, she wasn't attracted to either of them. Like, not at *all*. And yet, she couldn't help but feel like she was staring at a pair of puppies right now, the two of them doing their best to look completely pathetic . . . like a pair of defenceless *babies*. It would be cruel for her to turn them down.

What else was she meant to say? That she urgently needed to get to writing up her notes on the lecture they'd just had? Oh, sure, she *was* studying maths, after all, but that didn't mean that she would have to play right into the heart of the stereotype.

She could have a *drink* if she wanted to . . . of *course* she could.

So she said yes.

3

TARA WAS REGRETTING IT no sooner than five minutes later.

In fact, she'd already gone past the point of *regretting* and had moved onto the more logical steps of just how, exactly, she might be able to get out of the thing.

The bus rumbled around her like a mother bear, and even the light smell of burning coming from the heaters wasn't enough to put her off her thoughts. She was already thinking about *beer* and how it might *taste* . . . she had tried it a while back, when she'd gone to a pub with her parents. Her dad had ordered a *beer* and she'd decided to push the boat out and give it a try. As she recalled it, it had been bitter, a fairly unpleasant taste. The way she remembered the thing, it made her think of mushing a few slices of bread into a glass of water and then supping at them.

But there would be other drinks *besides* beer, wouldn't there?

And, anyway, she'd already resolved that she wasn't going.

The only question which remained was working out just *how*—exactly—she would manage to extract herself from the mess she'd got herself all toiled up in.

A text message? An email? A—*gasp*—phone call?

Tara couldn't quite put her finger on what would be the most acceptable method and, perhaps, as she realised as her bus pulled up to its spot in town, that was the reason why she ended up coming to the conclusion that there was no other option *but* to go and meet the boys.

4

I T WAS AROUND nine o'clock when Tara walked in through the door to the Ghat Inn—a pub only about five minutes away from her house. She had passed the place several times, of course, and each time given it an extremely wide berth. On Friday and Saturday nights, on her way back from the campus library, she would spot the bouncers on the doors—all bald and wearing long black jackets. And she would see the queue of people waiting to go in: the girls in their flimsy dresses and the boys in their shirts and jeans, and their buffed-up shoes.

She had always hurried on, got away from them, never wanting to accidently catch somebody's eye, find herself—*somehow*—catching an acquaintance's eye and getting hauled along into the place. For some reason, she'd built it up in her mind as a kind of nightmare scenario.

Tonight she had gone with a light-pink blouse—buttoned up to her throat—and a pair of sensible black jeans. She had also splashed on a little perfume—the name escaped her, but it smelled a little of elderberries. When she had headed out of the house, passed by the living room where her parents sat: her father with his nose buried in the newspaper while her mother did her cross-stitching; she'd hoped that she might be able to pass by unnoticed.

But it had been impossible.

As Tara had stuck her key into the front door, both of them had stirred and asked her where she was going, 'all dolled-up' as her father had put it with a wry grin.

So she had told them straight out, that she was off to go and meet up with a pair of boys.

That had brought on a silence.

But no complaints from either.

And Tara had taken her chance to slip out into the night.

Now she stood here, in the doorway of the Ghat Inn. It was a Tuesday so there weren't any men on the doors—no 'bouncers'—and the inside of the place seemed almost empty. Almost right away she spotted Paul and Thom, both of them sitting off in the corner. They were both wearing shirts, and she could see that Paul wasn't wearing a baseball cap and that he'd made some effort to comb and/or *wash* his hair.

Already feeling deeply subconscious, as if somebody might pop up before her and tell her that she didn't belong here, Tara scuttled along the floor over to the two of them.

The seats consisted of low stools with squishy cushions. She sat herself down on one of them and stared across the table at them. She saw that they both already had a drink sitting before them, and that both the drinks were now about a quarter full. She thought that it was beer inside the glass but she wouldn't have been able to say that with any conviction.

"So," Paul said, with a slight yawn, "You made it finally?"

Tara had consulted the internet for advice on coming on a date —this *was* a sort of date, wasn't it?—and it had suggested that she arrived 'fashionably late'. Since they'd made the appointment for eight thirty, she had deduced, taking a consensus, that arriving about half an hour later than scheduled would be perfectly acceptable.

But perhaps Paul and Thom read from a different rule sheet...

Thom gripped tight to his glass of beer(?) and glanced over the rim at her. "Are you feeling better now?"

"Huh?" Tara said.

With a slight smile, Paul made the motion of tears streaking his cheeks with his index finger.

"Oh," Tara said, for some reason only now remembering, "that was just something that was in my eye." She blinked a couple of times as if to demonstrate for them. "It's gone now," she added.

A long silence followed and Tara realised that, about the place, coming from *somewhere*, music leaked out from speakers. It was the steady grind of bass and drums which she'd hear when she picked the wrong radio station. She wondered how anybody could put up with that racket . . . or at least that was what her father would have said.

Did Thom and Paul listen to that music?

Paul finished off the remainder of his drink, as did Thom, and then he asked Tara what she wanted from the bar. Not really knowing what to order, she just asked Paul to get her the same of whatever it was that he was having.

That left Thom and Tara alone.

"So," Thom said, apparently trying to make conversation, "do you live with friends?"

Tara shook her head. "No, with my parents."

"Ha," Thom said, as if it was the first note of a laugh.

Tara stared down at her fingernails, and she wondered if she maybe should've had a scout around her bedroom for some varnish. Wasn't that what all the girls liked to do when they went 'out on the town?'

She found it tricky to make eye contact with people while she spoke to them, so she just kept staring at her fingernails when she said, "Where do you and Paul live?"

She looked up then, for no particular reason other than that it felt right.

Thom jerked his thumb over his shoulder, indicating only the wall of the bar, but which Tara deduced to mean *outside*. "Just around the corner," he said. "We share a house with a couple of others."

"Boys?" Tara said, surprising even herself at her forthrightness.

"Yeah," Thom said with a slight smile. "Just boys."

Paul returned from the bar with three glasses of the same liquid she had seen Thom and Paul drinking before. The slightly orange colour that she'd identified as being beer. Yes, in fact, she was pretty much certain of it . . . that it *was* beer.

Paul took up his seat once more. He slid the drinks to each of them.

Tara simply stared down into hers, already pretty certain that she could smell that familiar mouldy bread odour. It turned her gut just a little only thinking about it. She decided to restrict her breathing to only the odd little gasp here and there.

Thom glanced to Paul. "She said she lives with her parents still."

Paul rolled his eyes and then reached into the back pocket of his jeans. He brought out his wallet, flipped through a bunch of flaps and then withdrew a five-pound note which he handed over to Thom.

Thom took it with a grin and then, after taking his first sip of the beer, while slipping the note into his pocket, said, "He bet me you'd be living with friends."

"Oh," Tara said, widening her eyes a little and wondering why they would've made such an inane bet . . . then again, she supposed that only the truly *stupid* dedicated their lives to gambling.

5

THE NEXT FEW MOMENTS, again, were dedicated to silence, to the gentle sipping of their drinks, and, for Tara, the first sips of her own beer. It really was just about as revolting as she had recalled it. Not as much as like drinking bread as she had thought before . . . no, more like supping on rotten wood.

When she got done with her sip, she glanced about the bar. Only the sleepy barmen standing propped up at the counter chatting lazily. She felt as though somebody had just turned the music in the place up a little. Those thuds and grinds seemed louder to her . . . or maybe—*just maybe*—she was getting *drunk*.

She looked back down into her drink, into the *beer*, and she tried to fathom just how anybody could seriously drink this stuff for pleasure. But the whole matter escaped her. She was a logical thinker, after all, and the thought of people poisoning themselves on purpose just made no sense.

Like, at all.

The silence around the table continued until Paul broke it—he was now about halfway through his beer, and Thom only had about a quarter of his left.

"Want to dance?" Paul said.

His cheeks were a little flushed now, and his pupils—at least to Tara—seemed to have become dilated.

Tara looked about her. She couldn't see a dance floor anywhere. But did the music seem louder still? She glanced back down at her beer and decided that just about anything was better than having to suck back the rest of *that*.

With a vague smile, she said, "Okay."

Paul and Thom exchanged glances, and Tara couldn't help thinking that this question was deeply premeditated. They rose up off their stools and Tara did the same.

The dancing started out just like Tara saw on TV programmes from time to time, which was to say it was an odd collection of jerky movements of the arms mixed in with a strange swinging of the hips. She did her best to keep up with the boys, but really didn't find that she could go much past the basics. And, in any case, she felt somewhat self-conscious about the pair of barmen who were no doubt watching her as they polished up glasses.

Pretty soon, Tara was in the mood to go back home.

Indeed, when they sat back down again, she found herself staring into the amber liquid of her beer, and she knew that she simply wouldn't be able to drink another drop without puking all over the place.

She looked to the two boys and told them of her wishes.

Their expressions turned to a touch of disappointment, but she really couldn't think of any other way to communicate her desires. It simply wasn't worth hanging about here if she wasn't having fun, even for politeness' sake. And, anyway, hadn't the whole ruse for this invitation been geared towards making her feel better? Geared towards working out why it had been that she'd cried earlier on?

And so they headed out of the door to the bar and Tara found herself caught in the clutches of an awkward goodbye.

For some reason, Tara had always found goodbyes awkward.

There were the starter elements: limp-wristed wave, peck on the cheek, hug without the peck on the cheek . . . etcetera, etcetera . . . and then there was the conversation afterwards, or the decision whether to walk right away, or not.

And she found herself staring right in the face of a goodbye right now.

She really had no clue what she should do.

Thom and Paul looked fairly expectant so she supposed that should've given her an idea.

But she settled on the limp-wristed wave and turned away from them.

"See you tomorrow?" Thom said as she walked away from them with her back turned.

Tara kept walking, not bothering to look back. "Yes," she said.

As she turned the corner which led away from the bar, and left the two boys behind, she wondered what things *would* be like tomorrow. She guessed that, more or less, they would be the same. That she would have to struggle through another mechanics lecture.

Hopefully this time she wouldn't get something stuck in her eye—find herself on the receiving end of all that *attention.*

But, she supposed, just as long as nobody told her that she *wasn't* okay she would be fine.

Just fine.

TINY CHOW

TINY CHOW sat upright on the sofa. He arched his back to appear taller alongside Real Paul. Not Darwin stirred up a vodka tonic by the jukebox, a relic from the fifties, while Stir checked his hair in the mirror. The bass, from the stage next door, beat away at the walls. It pushed at the gently mashing beats that came from the small jukebox on the floor.

"Y'all, I don't see the trouble," Tiny Chow said, scratching at the part of his wrist covered by a gold bracelet. "I grown, see?"

"Ain't no doubt you grown," Not Darwin said. "Trouble being, we got the flyers made up, it's on the record, the people knows you as Tiny Chow, dog."

Stir backed up from the mirror, his hair slicked over to one side. "Listen to Darwin, man, he telling the truth."

Tiny Chow glanced at Real Paul whose head rolled back on his neck as he snored away. "I'd just like it if y'all would consider it."

"Course we will," Not Darwin said, taking a sip and then grimacing. He made them strong. "Gotta put it through the right channels, that's all."

"Right," Tiny said. "Suits, yeah?"

Not Darwin nodded, as if acknowledging a universal truth.

No one could change a universal truth.

Tiny knew it was about money. It had to be. That was what they did it for.

Why else?

He supposed some point in the past, when he lived in his grandmother's basement, the music had provided him some escapism. But the dreams of hot tubs full of bikinied models and rims that shone so bright he couldn't look at them directly were what kept him going.

"It just, I dunno." Tiny looked down into his lap. "I ain't no boy no more."

Not Darwin put his hands together in prayer and said, "We hear you, we hear you."

"What's wrong with just Chow, plain and simple?"

"Chow's good," Not Darwin said. "But it don't have the ring you get from the 'Tiny' part, you get me?"

"So y'all saying I can't change?" Tiny felt himself getting angrier. He wanted to punch the sleeping Real Paul in the stomach, wake him up real good. That would help a little. But instead of punching Real Paul, Tiny got to his feet and stood up to Not Darwin. It frustrated him that he had to bend his neck upwards to look him in the eye. "Listen! From this night on, I'm known as Chow, got me?" he said, imitating Not Darwin.

Not Darwin remained calm, his eyelids drooped down to half cover his eyes. "You'd best step down, little brother, or someone's gonna teach you a lesson."

Stir sidled up to Not Darwin's shoulder and cracked his knuckles.

Tiny remained resilient, staying where he was. If he backed down now his chance would be gone forever. "Know what the ladies do?" Tiny said, looking at the scar that ran across Not Darwin's face.

That attack had almost left him one eyed.

"No." Not Darwin looked amused.

Tiny held out his little finger and shook it at Not Darwin and Stir. "They do this, see?"

"Aw, come on boy." Not Darwin laid a hand on Tiny's shoulder.

Tiny thought better than to try to shake it off.

"We know that ain't true!" Tiny said.

Not Darwin laughed and Stir joined in.

Stir's chuckle annoyed Tiny. He had a portable DVD player and he spent the journeys on the tour bus chuckling away to himself. Tiny wanted to smack him, right in that squidged-up nose.

Real Paul grunted and turned over in his sleep, distracting them.

Tiny shrugged off Not Darwin's hand and sat back down on the sofa to sulk.

Bruno, their personal security, popped his head around the door. "Ten minutes max, boys. Crowd's getting real restless."

He went away again.

"Boy," Not Darwin said, "you'd best get your game face on, or there'll be trouble."

To Tiny, Not Darwin resembled a mountain. He wanted to take on the mountain. But it'd have to be some other time. He sighed.

There was no doubt who won that battle. Tiny hoped the war wasn't over, however, his pride was at stake.

Not Darwin slapped Real Paul's face a couple of times and Real Paul looked around, dopey from his snooze. "We on or what?" Real Paul said.

"Ten minutes," Not Darwin said. "And, Tiny?"

"Yeah?" Tiny said, not looking up from his high-top trainers.

"You doin' the routine tonight," Not Darwin said.

"Ah, what?" Tiny whipped his neck back and glared at Not Darwin, all the time aware that his expression was more pitiful than pit-bull. "It's so humiliating."

"Don't care, boy, you gotta learn some respect if you wanna roll with us." Not Darwin nodded at Real Paul. "You up for it right, Paul?"

"Sure, Darwin, whatever you say." Real Paul grinned at Tiny Chow, showing him his gold teeth.

All Tiny could do was shake his head and mutter "It ain't right" to himself over and over again.

Bruno came back. "Come on, boys, we on!"

Tiny bent down and put himself on Real Paul's shoulders. Paul hiked him to the sky. Tiny's head brushed the ceiling. The worst part was that he wasn't too big for this. It wasn't impossible for Real Paul to do this to him.

Not Darwin swaggered out the door, his chest now bare and rippling with greased-up muscles.

Stir smirked at Tiny as he followed him out.

Tiny Chow plotted. Perhaps he would have the last laugh after all. At least they gave him songs. That was something. It was a long road to respect, he knew that. Something he needed to earn like money, but harder. There was no buying it. The only way was hard slog: blood, sweat and tears; and this ritual embarrassment.

Who was he kidding? Maybe, he'd car bomb the lot of them motherfuckers, starting with that smug, squidged-up nose of Stir's. He knew a guy.

He could get it done tonight if he wanted.

He rocked back and forth on Real Paul's shoulders as his plan formed in his wicked brain.

He might get the front page.

ALL THESE ADORING
MULTITUDES

A CURTAIN of purple and pink lights blinked down onto the familiar lettering of the TV show title, filling out like a liquid pouring into a glass: Winners / Losers. It flashed several times, bathing the audience in its transient glow.

The presenter, Troy Lewis, stood off at the side, adjusting his shirt cuffs before sliding his hand through his well-greased black hair. He eyed the director's assistant, a clipboard clutched to her chest, waited for the signal and then ventured out, all teeth and shiny orange skin.

The audience roared in his ears, almost drowning out the director's voice in his earpiece. He approached his mark, arched his back, keeping his shoulders straight, and made eye contact with Row Seven, just like always.

"Welcome one and all to Winners and Losers!"

Another roar from the crowd.

Troy flushed through his opening monologue, sending the audience into stitches of laughter in all the correct places, and then he shifted back to his podium from which he welcomed the contestants onto the stage.

On autopilot, he reeled off their dreary occupations and mundane likes, and dislikes, before getting down to the show itself.

The show consisted of simple questions and answers posed alternately to each of the contestants. If the contestant's answer was correct, they were awarded a point. At the end of the show, the contestant with the most points won. In the case of a tie, there would be a sudden death round wherein the contestants would be asked questions in turn, the first to answer incorrectly declared the Loser, and the other, the Winner.

It was beautiful in its simplicity.

God how many times Troy had fended off producers' repeated

attempts to complicate the structure—adding in bonus rounds, options for further audience involvement or fiddling with the scoring system. There had even been once such instance where a producer had openly floated the suggestion of retirement. After over twenty-five years, Troy didn't just believe he was the reason for the continued success, for ratings holding steady in the internet age, he *knew* he was.

The one-thousand-and-sixty-fifth show passed like a dream. Banter rolled off Troy's tongue, tickling contestants and audience alike. He felt unstoppable. At the end of the show, he clapped his hands together, gave the audience his signatory signoff, "See you next time on Winners and Losers," and then strolled off the stage with the blanket of applause still warming his cheeks and sending his heart thudding.

His personal assistant, Anne, was already waiting with his lemon-scented, damp towel. He gave her a grin and a wink, then took the towel from her, pressing it to his forehead, feeling the veins in his brain whir and jolt. Only once he reached his dressing room could he really relax, with his own space, not another person in sight.

As he had done for the other one thousand and sixty-four shows, he sat in silence, staring into the mirror, watching the balls of sweat roll down his concealer-caked face until he had shucked off the high of being in front of an audience.

Later he could watch the show and relive the sensation. He kept a copy of each show on DVDs in his house, several bookcases dedicated to them.

There was a rapping at his dressing room door.

"Come in."

Anne peered around the door with a handful of letters. She strutted up to his chair and laid them out on the counter, where the makeup artist would lay her tools before the show. She stood at his shoulder like a subordinate officer.

He picked up the half dozen envelopes and leafed through them, picking out one which had particularly well-crafted handwriting. He turned it over, noting its torn flap—all his mail was searched through before Anne presented it to him—and tugged out the folded A5 paper, unfolding it with an eyebrow arched.

Although it had been written on unlined paper, the writer had clearly used some sort of a guide since the lines all flowed as one, never jerking or looping away from their invisible track. He read it over. There was a thick red cross scrawled at the top in marker pen.

Anne gasped. She reached to snatch the letter. "Oh, no, Mr Lewis, that one's not meant for you."

Troy ducked her reach, holding the letter down at his thigh. He eyed her. "Why ever not?"

"It's . . . it's—"

"Out with it, girl."

She grimaced, as if the admission physically pained her. "That's not a very nice letter."

"What're you talking about? I *only* receive nice letters. Only my fans bother to write in. If you're going to faff about, distracting me, I'd rather you left me in peace."

"But, sir, I'd really rather—"

He waved his hand. "Go on, buzz off."

She hesitated a moment, her eyes bulging like ping pong balls and then, reluctantly, beat her exit from the room, closing the door behind her.

Anne reminded Troy of a skittish animal, like those baby deer that would populate his family's country home. Whenever anyone got too close, the baby deer would visibly shake and then scamper away to its mother's teat.

Troy allowed himself a smile and a shake of the head as he pored over the letter:

Dear Mr Lewis,

I have frequently found myself watching your show during its afternoon slot, at four o'clock due to my aged mother's condition. She has lost her concentration, you see, and like a vegetable she will happily sit and watch any old thing that moves—rather like a kitten, in fact.

I write to you today to express my sincere displeasure with your show and its flimsy production. In this day and age it is hard to believe that something so trivial and nasty has carried on all these years unchecked.

Let us take your horrific makeup for a starting point. You blaze onto our screens, into our homes, with that computer-designed smile and paedophile's get-up expecting to soar into the hearts of middle-aged females.

It's despicable and distinctly ordinary.

Whenever I attempt to turn the channel away from your pseudo-youthful frolickings my mother gets herself all wound up into a state, screaming and scratching like a toddler. And as I have no choice but to sit there with her, lest she need something, I'm also forced to endure your drivel at high-volume (my mother is almost deaf).

That is why I write asking that you please, kindly, retire from the show and, preferably, hunch off to some far corner of the globe and hide out the rest of your days leaving us free to live out our lives without your horrendous, unwanted presence.
Failing that, just plug up the openings in your garage and gas yourself to death with your car exhaust.

I sincerely doubt this will make it through whatever censors you place between yourself and your 'fans' but in the event it does, I hope that you take heed of my words. This isn't a joke. I really, and truly, hate your guts and wish you a calm and speedy (but not necessarily painless) death.

Yours,

Clifford Hill (not a fan)

A strange quivering sensation took hold of Troy's body. His blood pumped faster and his palms sweated. He placed the letter down on the makeup rack and gazed into the mirror, looking deep into his eyes. Never, in all his life, had he received such a barrage of abuse. Occasionally, when out in public, people would shout things—but they were innocuous: 'orange-face', 'greaser' or, at worse, 'cunt'.

But all those comments went unheeded and he believed—*nay*, knew—they were posed to him from the depths of thickly-formed jealousy. But this, this letter, was quite different. It was well-argued, contained, largely grammatically correct, and, in short, a biting dress down of his faults.

There was a tentative knock at his door.

He let out a grunt, which could have been interpreted any of a million different ways.

Anne slipped into the room, a nervous smile on her lips. "You . . . You read the letter?"

"Yes."

She stepped closer. "And, well, what would you like me to do with it?"

"Do I receive a lot of letters like these, Anne?"

"Oh, of course not, Mr Lewis. Why that must be some kind of joke."

It felt like he was sinking down into the upholstery. The sensation reminded him of when he had once felt nervous at the prospect of doing his shows, like he was in some way fallible.

He hadn't felt like this in years and he despised the feeling.

He turned in his chair, keeping his focus fixed on the floor, the cream-coloured tiles, well-polished every evening so that they glinted in the light from the mirror lamps. "Please. Tell me the truth."

"Sir, you know how it is. You receive hundreds of letters a day. You couldn't possibly respond to each of them personally."

"Yes, I quite understand that. But what I want to know is whether or not you exercise some kind of 'censorship' "—it burnt his throat to use the diction of the letter writer—"on what I receive?"

"Oh, well—"

He sneered. "You know, play a game of 'Give Troy all the good news, none of the bad', 'Keep him sweet, keep him stupid' ?"

"Mr—"

He slammed his fist into the makeup rack. The letter brushed off and fell to the floor, arcing back and forth as it floated downward, like a leaf falling from a tree. "For fuck's sake! Tell me the truth."

She flinched.

Troy knew, from experience, that using profanity somewhat grated against his image of the squeaky-clean, afternoon-game-show-host profile, but, having read that letter—found out that somewhere out there people didn't like—no—openly *hated* him—there was no other way to express himself succinctly, rationally.

Anne's mouse-like features, her twitching nose and fragile jaw, seemed to float about her delicate skin. She drew her lips into a tight and puckered 'oh'.

Troy stared at the letter that now lay at his feet, the clean and neatly-measured lines peering back up at him like some kind of gremlin. "I'm sorry, Anne, I didn't mean to frighten you." He swallowed, leant over in his chair and picked the letter up, reading it over again, mouthing each of the words.

When he had finished the second reading, he glanced over it, and then checked the envelope. Not finding what he required, he turned his attention to Anne. "Say, does this gentleman have a return address on file?"

"Generally the writers of these sorts of letters don't leave a return address."

"But could we find it out if required?"

Anne fidgeted with the trim of her blouse, obviously afraid at what she might be getting herself involved with.

"Well?" he said.

"There is a procedure which we use to ascertain the addresses of unmarked letters. Yes, we could find out the return address. But, I really don't think that would be a good idea, after all—"

Troy held up his hand. "I'd like you to go put the wheels into motion right away, get this chap's address for me."

She stepped forward. "Mr Lewis, if it's a case of—"

"Look, I'm not angry. I just want to understand this person, meet him in real life. Can you just do this task for me? I promise that I won't hold you responsible in any way. This is just something which I want to follow up alone."

"Yes, sir."

"Good."

She slipped past him, picked up the letter and envelope and then made for the exit.

"Anne?"

"Yes?"

"What's my schedule like for tomorrow? Any filming?"

"Not until Friday, sir."

"Other engagements?"

"I believe you have a visit to a cancer clinic booked in."

"Cancel it."

"Very well, sir."

"And have the city car filled up, will you? Think it was running low last time I took it out."

She stepped out into the corridor and, through the closing door, said, "Of course."

Troy straightened in his chair, looking himself in the eye, in the mirror. The 'city car' was the vehicle he and his wife used to go about town when they didn't want to draw attention to themselves, when they went shopping or visited restaurants. He wouldn't dream of turning up at this man's house in his Rolls, that would only infuriate him further—seeing the success that accompanied him. No, if he were going to convince him he would have to be humble and diplomatic.

The next day, around mid-morning, Troy slopped down the rest of his café latte and then tossed the empty cup into the floor space of the passenger side of the car. He tapped the address of his hate mailer into his smartphone, held in place on the dashboard by a sucker, and then turned the key in the ignition.

On his way out of High Birth Gardens, a gated community, he waved to the widow, Mrs Norris. She wore a purple dress and straw sunhat as she crouched down, seeing to her petunias.

Her husband had invented a new form of searching for oil deposits, for which he had been handsomely paid. Mrs Norris herself was a deep-seated fanatic of Troy's shows, and he always made a point of sending her signed photographs every so often.

Keep the neighbours sweet, etcetera . . .

She waved to him and he rolled down the window, and drew to

a halt at the curb. Wiping her hands on the sides of her dress, she approached the car, her lips a golden orange today. "Good morning, Mr Lewis. Are you off filming today?"

"No, going to see a fan, actually."

She gave him a wink. "Oh, that sounds like the diamond service."

Often he had received offers from female fans, women in their fifties, and it wasn't particularly any respect for his wife which kept him from completing the conquests, more the fact that he wasn't all that interested in sex. The whole act was messy, physically and emotionally, and just so overrated. He preferred nice and clean Power and Respect.

And if a squeaky clean image accompanied his chastity, all the better.

He smiled, presuming that Mrs Norris was flirting with him. "Nothing like that, it's a man out on the other side of the town. He watches the show with his ill mother."

"Sounds like a good boy, nothing like my children, I'll tell you. Every time they come around they're looking at their watches, just praying for time to spin on, can't wait to get away. No time for their mother."

Although he tried to resist, he couldn't prevent himself glancing at the clock on his smartphone. These days off were problematic. He knew that he had the whole day to burn, but he always had a nagging feeling that he had to cherish every second, not waste it chin-wagging with some *acquaintance*.

He rested his hands on the wheel. "Suppose you'll be watching this afternoon."

"You know me, Mr Lewis. I wouldn't dream of missing an episode."

"My number one fan."

She blushed slightly. "I'll let you go on your way, then."

He nodded and then crushed the accelerator pedal, and drove

on out through the electric gates, which flew open without the slightest creak or groan.

He headed out on the motorway, eating up the countryside with the radio on in the background.

There was some discussion about a football player being paid three times the natural GNP of some African country he couldn't pronounce, let alone point out on a map, and the presenters were in an uproar about it. Although Troy despised football, and sport in general, he kept on listening in, trying to see how he might adapt the discussion to his own situation:

The female presenter, whom he imagined as a leggy brunette, late-twenties, said, "I just cannot believe in this globalised day and age we're stuck here having this conversation. It's just ridiculous what happens on one side of the planet, while the other suffers."

The male presenter, whom he believed to be a grey fox, something of another version of himself, replied, "What you've got to understand is that this all depends on supply and demand. People like to watch football, lots of people, and they're prepared to pay good money for it. Is it anyone's fault but the public's that these clubs take advantage of them, charge them a small fortune for tickets to fund their players' fat salaries?"

"But surely there must be another way," the woman replied. "The players could club together their wages and put it toward something more worthwhile."

"Let me give you a personalised example. Imagine that another radio station offered you forty times the salary to go and do the same job you do day in day out, with a larger audience? What would you say to that?"

"I'd probably accept."

"Right, and then what would happen with your wages?"

"Well, I might set up a charity, put some money aside every month for a worthy cause."

"Ah, but do you really believe that would change anything, make an impact on the world? What you have to understand is that these people just don't live in the real world. They probably see all of life's problems and feel overwhelmed with the scale, and so they spend their money thriftlessly on cars, wine, women . . . do you see?"

"In a way, I mean . . ."

Troy's smartphone blinked at him, indicating that he had to take the next turn. He reached out and turned down the radio. His brain was constructed as such that he found it near enough impossible to do more than one thing at once, especially when one of the tasks involved following directions.

His sense of time and space was well out of whack.

He spun through a few roundabouts and got himself on the indicated road, which led along a winding suburban sprawl. Keeping both hands on the wheel, his ears pricked for the next instruction from his smartphone, he drove on.

The smartphone indicated the turn up ahead. Troy spun the wheel and shot down the cul-de-sac, taking note of the house numbers. Clifford Hill lived at number twenty-six. He read off the numbers and pulled up at the appropriate one.

Troy sat in the car a few moments, considering the façade of the house. It was a semi-detached house with a horribly sixties gravel-scrub pressed into its walls. Netted curtains kept a semblance of modesty for the pair of windows facing into the street. There was a boxy blue car sat in the driveway, a large dent just behind the petrol cap.

He doubted it did over fifty miles an hour.

He flicked off his seatbelt, took a deep, cleansing breath and then stepped out of the car, and into the fray. He marched up the path, preparing his smile and trying to get a hold of his beating heart.

It hurt to admit it, but he was quite terrified of what might befall him with this hater.

He delivered a pair of smart knocks and then stood back to wait.

From within the house there was a whiny, undistinguishable shout, and then the scruff of footfall brushing a carpet. The door swung open and a large, bald man squinted back at him. He wore a white vest and a pair of jeans which swooped so low as to reveal the early tufts of public hair just below his bellybutton.

Clifford Hall.

He blinked a couple of times and then his jaw dropped. He pointed an accusing finger. "You're . . . Troy Lewis."

Troy couldn't prevent himself from flashing his eyebrows and then holding his hands up as if in surrender, just like he did on the game show.

"Wh . . . What the hell are you doing here?"

"I got your letter."

"Oh."

Troy peered beyond him, into the gloomy house. "Is your mother at home?"

"Uh, oh, yeah, of course she is. Just in the sitting room."

"May I . . . ?"

Clifford ducked back inside, giving Troy room to squeeze past.

It was a narrow corridor with a wooden shelf which was overflowing with letters, all piled up one on top of the another. There was a small ornamental deer prancing forth beside them. The edges of its base were chipped. The house smelled of musk and chicken soup.

Troy tried to slow his breathing, to ward off the foul odour. He indicated the doorway to his left. "In here, is she?"

Clifford nodded, his mouth slightly ajar and expression gormless.

Troy padded into the sitting room. It was dark despite the fairly bright day outside. He thought it might be because of the brown wallpaper. If he had come to live in a place like this—God forbid—that would've been the first to go.

He took in the rest.

A sofa, battered and faded, the woman, Clifford Hall's mother, sat with her back to him, the back of her grey-haired head bobbing up and down as she watched some programme or other.

Troy rounded the sofa, took a seat on a chair opposite her, and held up his hands to frame his face, giving her his best smile.

She turned her head slowly from the TV screen and met his gaze. Her lips trembled and then her mouth opened, eyes glazing over. "It's you."

"That's right."

And then she fainted.

When Clifford had brought his mother around, explaining all the time that she was frail to surprises and on various different kinds of medication, he offered Troy a cup of tea and some biscuits, which Troy chomped his way through contentedly. Clifford's mother, it seemed, had got over her shock and was now thoroughly engrossed in the TV screen, as if she had forgotten that Troy was there at all.

The programme featured a pair of contestants attempting to sell their heirlooms at auction. The auctioneer-cum-presenter was Nigel Pimplebee. Troy knew him well. He was infamous for his Christmas parties, which took place out at his country mansion. That was the only time when Troy would really allow himself to get drunk, lose control, and only because everyone else was so far gone—and they were so *far* away from the city—that they wouldn't remember anything that happened there.

Once Troy had finished his tea and permitted himself a biscuit, which he would have to burn off that evening in his home gym, he decided the moment was right to confront Clifford over the letter.

As it was a matter of utmost sensitivity, another man's opinion, he had to treat it with due care. Nonetheless he did feel a flush of anger as he thought back over those harsh words, those undignified and extreme suggestions. He brushed biscuit crumbs from his lap, set himself straight on and looked Clifford in the eye. "About this letter, then?"

Clifford's attention remained half on the TV screen, but he gave Troy the dignity of a slight glance. "Erm, yes."

"I read it over. Twice. And I decided to come here today to ask you straight out about it. There's some pretty harsh things that you've said there, considering we've never once met in real life, until now. So, what have you got to say about it?"

Clifford's Adam's apple bobbed in his throat. "I . . . I just felt I had to tell you how I felt. It's not fair that you keep on going through with the same charade over and over again. You're tricking my mum, there's something of a drug about you, keeping her addicted. She can't miss an episode."

"If you find my presence so offensive, why not change the channel?"

"Well, it's like I said in the letter, Mum won't allow it. She'll scream the bloody house down before she lets me."

"Perhaps it's because I provide something for your mother which you cannot provide for her yourself."

Clifford coloured a touch. This time he turned all his attention onto Troy. His hand wandered his thigh, picked out a patch of leg and scratched. "Look, I don't enjoy what I do, but it's an obligation I can't walk away from. All I wanted to put across in that letter is how much I hate you and your bloody programme, is it a problem to permit me that little piece of bile?"

Troy straightened in his seat. "Yes, well, I think I can see that your issues are personal, rather than my own."

"But you're the one who set them off, the one who continues going out there, day after day, with your plastic face and clingy contestants forcing us all to watch you go about the mundane display. Don't you have other interests? Things you want to achieve in your life? God knows, if I had the money and freedom, I would do what I wanted."

"I have no idea what you're talking about, I have plenty of free time."

"So you do just see the game show as a job?"

Troy's mind flickered back over the years and years he had put into Winners and Losers. It was hard to imagine what would take that space in his life. All these years he had really wanted to go off and climb mountains, sail tossing oceans, but the programme schedule, let alone his insurance, wouldn't cover those costs, and he hadn't wanted to go out on a bad note, leaving his wife behind with a ton of debt in his name.

Bad press.

If there was one thing he feared in life, it was that in death his name would get sullied and he wouldn't be able to come to his own defence. Nonetheless, the question remained: had he really done everything he had wanted in his life?

"Well?" Clifford said. "Are you really proud of what you've achieved in your life? Whenever I flick over to your game show, have to endure those fucking sparkly lights and polite applauses, I think about all that money and power you've got, and the little you do with it."

"I think you'll find I'm the patron of several charities—"

Clifford snorted, sneering. "Bollocks to all that. I'm talking about real achievements. If I'd had the chance, not got laid off from my job to look after Mum, I would be off out seeing the world right now. Every time I see you, others like you, it pains me to think of what opportunities you have to change the world and you pass them up."

"I . . . I . . ." Troy started, but, for the first time in his life, he was rendered speechless, because he knew what Clifford said was true.

Clifford's smirk slipped from his lips and his eyes wandered back to the TV screen, where the lunchtime news was wrapping up. "That's why I said those things in the letter, and I believe and stand by each one of them. If you're not going to do anything on this spinning mass of rock, why not just step off and give room to someone who will?"

Troy sat there, steeped in silence. Clifford's mother let out a long and loud snore which sent a shudder along his skin. The advertisements rattled off on the TV. Only when Troy glanced at his smartphone, to check the time, did he realise that his show was coming on next. It wouldn't be right to hang around. He clearly wasn't welcome in this house, the whole episode had been a disaster from start to finish.

He rose from his seat.

Clifford turned to him. "You off, Mr Lewis?"

"Uh, I . . . I was just—"

"Really, it's fine. Go. Thanks for coming out to visit Mum. If she had any wits about her then I would say it meant something to her, but she won't remember a thing about it."

Troy nodded, searched for some suitable expression to say goodbye but failed, and beat a retreat down the corridor, with the familiar sound of the opening music of his game show in his ears.

Troy bombed down the motorway, his speedometer nudging ninety miles per hour. He just wanted to get home, have his daily glass of red wine a few hours early and then sit back on the sofa, not thinking of anything in particular.

Clifford's words rattled his brain, about how he was wasting his life doing what he did. It made Troy smile to think about it. How that man could believe he had any right to dish out advice, especially to someone as successful as Troy was, just beggared belief.

He downshifted as he rocked into a series of road works. The orange lights placed atop the traffic cones blinked in series, flashing from front to back. It was like he was back in the studio, awaiting another show. Twenty-five years. That was a long time in any profession, but in TV it seemed a lifetime.

But had it been a lifetime well spent?

When he got back home, making a point of speeding up as he came to Mrs Norris's house, he sipped at his glass of wine in his empty house—his wife had left a note that she had gone out shopping, getting ahead of the Christmas rush. He threw over all the thoughts in his mind and then picked up the phone and dialled his producer.

The line purred away in his ear. He cleared his throat several times and, finally, his producer picked up. "Troy?" his producer said. "See the show this afternoon?"

"Yes, I mean, no, I didn't."

"Ah, everything all right?"

"I was wondering about my leave, taking a break."

"What are you talking about?"

"From the show, I'd like to take some time off."

There was some muttering in the background. His producer came back. "Whatever for?"

Troy winced, squinted into his empty glass where a trace of wine lingered around the base. He glanced out the window at the perfectly trimmed hedges and gleaming cars. He had made a television studio of his life, everything calculated, wholly-imagined and executed.

"... Troy? Are you there?"

"Yes. I just have some things I'd like to do. You know, travel, go off to see the world."

"Well, how long? A week? Two weeks?"

"Um, I hadn't thought about when I'd come back."

His producer sighed. "You haven't missed a week your whole career."

"I know that."

"And now you're telling me that you might be away for longer? Look, Troy, you know how the business is. I can't tell you what you need, but I can tell you that things change quickly. On top of all that, the ratings for the show haven't been spectacular this season to be honest. I can't guarantee that, if you disappear for a few months, there'll be a show to come back to."

Outside, Troy watched a bird land on a tree branch. That was something else he had always wanted to get interested in: bird watching. His father had always been a fanatic, shelves stuffed full of bird spotting guides and identification diagrams. Those books were still in the house somewhere, probably in a box up in the loft.

He turned things over in his mind. He had enough money to reasonably retire. He had a profile to fall back on if he really did want to make a comeback, although it looked increasingly likely that he would never want to go back to TV.

Following the conversation this afternoon, everything else just blurred into insignificance.

"So, Troy? What've you got to say?"

"Just give me a moment, all right? I'll call back in a bit."

"Okay, then, let me know sooner rather than later, right?" There was a note of real concern in his producer's voice now.

Troy clicked the phone off and laid it down on the kitchen counter. He continued to watch the bird, twitching and twittering on the branch. And then, in a single, fluid movement, it flipped into the air, barrelled upwards and out of sight.

He looked to the phone and then snatched it up, tapping the autodial for his producer.

UNCLE VICTOR

THE VELVET DRAPES tumbled down onto the beige, woven carpet. Candlelight flickered, dampening the edges of the dining room with shadow. Family members, twenty-four in all, propped themselves up and chattered as they dug through their holiday meal: seared salmon with a variety of garnishes. Wine splashed into glasses before disappearing down long, bony throats. The children were in bed and it was time for the adults to shine.

Victor felt thoroughly out of place. He wore a green tweet jacket, punctuated by the odd tear and missing several of its brown buttons. His hair sprouted up in tufts. He had patted it down over his fringe to cover the alcoves of retreating hair at either side of his forehead. He sat down one end of the table, one seat away from the head, and he cut his way through his meal, doing his best not to raise his eyes from his plate.

The sooner this banquet was over with the better.

Cousin Henrietta, however, had other plans. Like everyone else in the family she was twig-thin. The collar of her blouse popped up through the neckline of her sweater, and a strand of pearls hung around her neck. She popped a piece of salmon in her mouth, chewed it around forty times and then gazed across the table at Victor. "What was it you said you were doing again?"

"Insurance," Victor said, not looking up, frantically cutting off another piece.

"Ah. And is that interesting?"

"I don't mind it."

"Ah," Henrietta said, smiling then returning to her plate.

Further on up the table, Grandpa Toby sneezed. A chorus of bless yous trotted over to him. Toby seized a napkin in his fist and blew into it. His cheeks reddened and sweat collected in pools between the wrinkles on his forehead.

Victor considered that a heart attack might be just what the dinner party needed to be livened up. Grandpa Toby was now into his nineties and Victor reckoned that the whole family kept sweepstakes on just how long he might last.

When the kerfuffle over the sneezing had died down, Henrietta turned her attention back to Victor. "And you haven't met a nice girl or anything?"

These dinners always ended up making him feel glum and depressed. Victor slurped some wine. "No."

"That's a pity."

"Yes."

Henrietta smiled at him then took some of her own wine.

Victor suppressed the urge to sigh and concentrated on his half-full wine glass. He had finished his meal now but still felt famished. The servants wouldn't bring any more. Second servings weren't on. He had no idea why he always returned here, whenever he got an invitation, as if it might be more interesting that the year before.

Auntie Miriam leant over her position at the head of the table, to Victor's side, to speak with Uncle Horace. The bases of her surgically-enlarged breasts scuffed the cream table cloth. Victor had always thought there might be something going on between Miriam and Horace. Interfamily marriage and partner switching was rife among his upper class family—an upper class family like his, in any case.

Something inside him tickled. The wine? Perhaps. Maybe it was the boredom seizing control of his limbs, some kind of reflex as his body attempted to ward off rigor mortis. Dessert wouldn't arrive for another twenty minutes or so. Coffee for an hour. He had to do something. No point just sitting staring at his wine.

He cleared his throat, met Henrietta's eye. "Um, I've got a joke. Would you like to hear it?"

As if someone had pre-empted his suggestion, there was a roar of laughter up the table. The unmistakable, haughty laugh of Great Uncle Cuthbert. A real echoing and resounding boom for such a skinny man.

Henrietta propped her elbows on the table and shunted forward in her seat. "Go on then."

Already Victor was having second thoughts. First things first, he wasn't the best joke-teller in the universe, and, second, the joke which had sprung to mind was a little on the controversial side. One of his salesmen, Jack, had told him it on Friday.

A smile twitched at the corner of his mouth as he recalled it.

Henrietta smiled back. "Tell me, please."

"Okay," Victor said, lowering his voice and eyeing Auntie Miriam, still swept up in conversation with Uncle Horace. "So, yesterday, I was talking to my girlfriend and she tells me that she's breaking up with me because I'm a zoophile."

Henrietta's eyes widened a touch and she cocked her head to one side. "A zoophile?"

Alarm bells rang for Victor. He thought about stopping but knew that he had to finish. "Uh, uh . . . so, then she, no, I say that, uh"—his palms got clammy and a knot formed in his gullet—"I say . . . it's awfully impressive to see a donkey speaking, let alone saying such a big word."

"A donkey? What's a big word?" Henrietta said, frown lines sketched in her forehead.

A tremble passed through Victor. He realised that Auntie Miriam and Uncle Horace were staring. When he glanced to his side he noticed the rest of the table was too. Everyone was steeped in silence.

Victor licked moisture into his bloodless lips. "Uh . . . uh . . . 'zoophile.'"

Someone down the table gasped.

Someone else asked, "What did he say?"

Someone repeated, " 'Zoophile.'"

" 'Zoophile' ?"

"That's right."

"What's that?"

"Someone who has sex with animals, I suppose."

All the muscles in Victor's jaw froze up and he concentrated on his empty plate, praying that a servant would appear in the dining room and break the stasis, the all-consuming silence.

Having recuperated from his earlier sneeze, Grandpa Toby got to his feet and looked down upon Victor. "You say that you're a zoophile."

A chill ran down Victor's neck. "No, no, no—"

Henrietta blinked her beady eyes. "That was what you said."

"No," Victor said. "It was a joke. Just a joke."

More muttering between the family. Finally a servant appeared out of the woodwork and set about collecting up empty plates, stooped to pour out more glasses of wine. However the damage had been done, no way could something so trivial as a *servant* distract from what was occurring.

Someone said, "He was playing with my dog this afternoon."

"And mine," someone else said.

Grandpa Toby tilted his head back, in imitation of the portrait of Sir Henry of Frotherwheel which hung in the hall of the country home. His features darkened and his skin took on a golden hue in the candlelight. "I should take it upon myself to call the police."

"Yes," someone said. "Call the police!"

Glasses clinked and the groan of conversation crept into life.

Victor wished to suddenly discover the secret to teleportation or, failing that, invisibility. But, of course, fate had no ear for his request.

Great Uncle Cuthbert rose to his feet, beside Grandpa Toby. "What makes you think it's appropriate to mention something like that at a celebration of our family? You . . . you're ill, demented, completely." Cuthbert balled his fists.

Grandpa Toby laid a hand on his shoulder and helped him back into his chair. Once he'd done so, he turned his attention back to Victor. "Well? What do you have to say for yourself?"

"I . . . I—"

"Stand up and face me like a man!" Grandpa Toby said.

Victor did as he was told. "It was a joke. Someone told me a joke."

Grandpa Toby flashed his eyebrows. "A joke?"

"Yes, yes," Victor said, nodding so much it made him dizzy.

"Perhaps you would enlighten us?"

Victor felt his stomach churn, digesting the salmon and wine, as he reeled through the joke another time. When he got to the end he took deep gulps of air and tried to relax, telling himself that now, finally, he would be understood.

Grandpa Toby listened throughout with his fingers pressed to his temple, in imitation of Lord Rutherford in the portrait that hung in the library, then said, "You're saying that you have a relationship with a donkey?"

Victor suppressed a groan. "No, it's imaginary. That's part of the joke."

"Part of the joke?" Auntie Miriam said, with a snort.

"Yes."

Auntie Miriam continued, "Wouldn't it make more sense, be less likely to be misunderstood, if you were to tell it in the third person?"

Mumbles of agreement rippled around the table.

"I . . . I suppose so," Victor said.

Great Uncle Cuthbert lurched from his chair, thrusting his finger in the air. "I don't care what he says, I'm calling the police, right this moment."

Grandpa Toby took the liberty to re-explain exactly what

Victor had just outlined for them. At first Cuthbert was adamant that he would call the police and it took another relative to persuade him back down into his chair.

Grandpa Toby stared long and hard at Victor, as if he were a worm he had just encountered in the crotch of his freshly-pressed riding jodhpurs, then he returned to his cushioned seat and immersed himself with some distant cousin.

Victor slumped back in his chair, staring at the curly cornices which lined the ceiling.

Throughout the rest of the dinner he stayed silent, accepting the pudding from the servant without comment before ploughing his way through it. He had half a mind to sneak out before coffee was served but he knew that would just exacerbate the situation. He would look guilty and despite the fact that it had just been a joke—a theorem to break the mundanity of the evening—the rest of the family would speak of him as a zoophile.

Forever more he could be pasted with that brush.

He thought over his appearance: the tattered jacket, the unkempt hair and he realised how his family, those supposedly closest to him—at least biologically—had needed no more than a pretext to point a modern day witch hunt in his direction. When he got back home the first thing he would do was find a new wardrobe.

Next, a wife.

One could never be too careful when it came to appearances.

As the evening wound down and Great Uncle Cuthbert fell asleep with his head resting on his placemat, Grandpa Toby called an ending to proceedings.

The guests all gathered their hats and coats from the cloakroom, ably assisted by the various servants whom Grandpa Toby employed, and then, one by one, they left through the Great Hall, shaking Grandpa Toby's hand as they went.

Victor lined up with the rest of them. The combination of the wine, nerves and his faux pas squeezed his sweat glands and dampened his spine. He counted off the members of his family wishing Grandpa Toby goodbye as they filed out to their valet-fetched cars.

When Victor rolled up in front of Grandpa Toby, a frown appeared on Grandpa Toby's lips. He craned his neck over Victor's shoulder and his whiskers itched Victor's cheek. "That was really quite a bad showing, young man."

"Yes," Victor said. "I'm so sorry."

Grandpa Toby rocked back on his heels, looked Victor up and down then, remaining serious, he clamped his enormous paw around Victor's hand, crushing every nerve in it, and then nodded to him. "I suppose we're to expect you for the dinner next year?"

If Grandpa Toby's comments carried an undertone it evaded Victor completely and he found himself grinning back in reply. "Oh yes, wouldn't dream of missing it."

"Drive safely."

Victor relinquished himself of Grandpa Toby's grip and made his way down the marble steps where his battered, old hatchback awaited him, a tuxedoed valet standing sentient with the keys dangling from his fingers.

Victor considered whether or not he really would be welcomed back.

One thing was for sure, that whatever happened he *would* be back—if only to save face and show his family that he was more than a social misstep.

And there was a certain loathing amongst his pragmatism.

AUTHOR'S NOTE

Thank you for taking the time to read one of my books. If you would like to hear about my latest releases you can sign up for my newsletter here: www.tjbainz.com

Thanks for reading!

TJ Bainz

Kindness And Happenstance
A Short Story Collection

www.ingramcontent.com/pod-product-compliance
Lightning Source LLC
Chambersburg PA
CBHW020948260626
47169CB00006B/1875